Alex shrugged. "I don't usually take women to armed robberies."

Now things were getting *interesting,* Bess thought. "Where *do* you take them?"

His gaze locked on hers. "To dinner, the flicks, dancing. To bed."

"Well, armed robbery is probably more exciting— at least than the first three." She rose, placed her hands on his shoulders and kissed him lightly on the mouth. "No hard feelings." When his hands came to her hips and held her in place, she lifted a brow. "Was there something else?"

His lips twitched. "I haven't decided yet. Maybe we could start with dinner."

"Start what?"

"Working our way to bed. That's where I want you."

"Oh." Her breath came out a little too quickly, and not quite steady. It didn't help that his eyes were calm, amused and very confident. How had their positions been so neatly reversed? "Well, *that's* certainly cutting to the chase...."

Dear Reader,

This March brings you a very special event—the publication of *Convincing Alex,* by Nora Roberts. This extraspecial SILHOUETTE SPECIAL EDITION title is the fourth tale in Nora's bestselling THOSE WILD UKRAINIANS series, and features Alex Stanislaski—definitely the sexiest detective in New York! Don't miss this wonderful story—it's destined to become a classic!

The March selection of our THAT SPECIAL WOMAN! promotion is *One Last Fling!* by Elizabeth August. This warm, wonderful tale is sure to win hearts! Our THAT SPECIAL WOMAN! series is a celebration of our heroines—and the wonderful men that they fall in love with.

This month also brings you stories from more of your favorite authors—Emilie Richards, Diana Whitney and Trisha Alexander—as well as a super debut book in the Special Edition lineup by Kate Freiman. A wonderful March will be had by all!

I hope that you enjoy this book and all of the stories to come.

Sincerely,

Tara Gavin
Senior Editor

Please address questions and book requests to:
Reader Service
U.S.: P.O. Box 1325, Buffalo, NY 14269
Canadian: P.O. Box 1050, Niagara Falls, Ont. L2E 7G7

Nora Roberts

NEW YORK TIMES BESTSELLING AUTHOR

CONVINCING ALEX

Silhouette®

SPECIAL ▼ EDITION®

Published by Silhouette Books
America's Publisher of Contemporary Romance

For Pat Gaffney,
to even things out

 SILHOUETTE BOOKS

ISBN 0-373-09872-3

CONVINCING ALEX

Copyright © 1994 by Nora Roberts

Printed in U.S.A.

NORA ROBERTS

is one of Silhouette Books's most popular and prolific authors, as well as a *New York Times* bestseller. Demand for early titles has been so great, they are being brought back as part of a special "Language of Love" collection.

Nora was the first author inducted into the Romance Writers of America's Hall of Fame and has received awards for her fiction, her creativity, her sales and her contribution to the genre. She has received lifetime achievement awards from the Romance Writers of America, Waldenbooks and *Romantic Times* magazine, as well as bestselling title and series awards from booksellers, readers and peers.

Nora Roberts is a consummate storyteller. Her generous spirit, humor, creativity, willingness to take chances and commitment to her characters, her writing and, most especially, her readers, have earned her fame worldwide.

THE STANISLASKI FAMILY TREE

Spencer Kimball m. Angela Winthrop (d.)

Frederica :

Natasha & Anthony Marshall

1st m. :Lily (d.)

2nd m.

Brandon

Katherine

Mikhail m. Sydney Hayward

Griffin

Alexi

Rachel m. Zackary Muldoon

Yuri Stanislaski
m.
Nadia Malenkov

LEGEND:
m.— married
d.— deceased

Chapter One

The curvy blonde in hot-pink spandex tottered on stiletto heels as she worked her corner. Her eyes, heavily painted with a sunburst of colors, kept a sharp watch on her associates, those spangled shadows of the night. There was a great deal of laughter on the street. After all, it was springtime in New York. But beneath the laughter there was a flat sheen of boredom that no amount of glitter or sex could disguise.

For these ladies, business was business.

After popping in some fresh gum, she adjusted the large canvas bag on her bare shoulder. Thank God it was warm, she thought. It would be hell to strut around half-dressed if the weather was ugly.

A gorgeous black woman in red leather that barely covered the essentials languidly lit a cigarette and cocked her hip. "Come on, baby," she said to no one in particular, in a voice husky from the smoke she exhaled. "Wanna have some fun?"

Some did, Bess noted, her eyes skimming the block. Some didn't. All in all, she thought, business was pretty brisk on this spring night. She'd observed several transactions, and the varied ways they were contracted. It was too bad boredom was the byword here. Boredom, and a defiant kind of hopelessness.

"You talking to yourself, honey?"

"Huh?" Bess blinked up into the shrewd eyes of the black goddess in red leather who had strolled over. "Was I?"

"You're new?" Studying Bess, she blew out smoke. "Who's your man?"

"My . . . I don't have one."

"Don't have one?" The woman arched her ruthlessly plucked brows and sneered. "Girl, you can't work this street without a man."

"That's what I'm doing." Since she didn't have a cigarette, Bess blew a bubble with her gum. Then snapped it.

"Bobby or Big Ed find out, they're going to mess you up." She shrugged. After all, it wasn't her problem.

"Free country."

"Girl, ain't nothing free." With a laugh, she ran a hand down her slick, leather-covered hip. "Nothing at all." She flicked her cigarette into the street, where it bounced off the rear fender of a cab.

There were dozens of questions on Bess's lips. It was in her nature to ask them, but she remembered that she had to go slow. "So who's *your* man?"

"Bobby." With her lips pursed, the woman skimmed her gaze up and down Bess. "He'd take you on. A little skinny through the butt, but you'd do. You need protection when you work the streets." And she could use the extra money Bobby would pass her way if she brought him a new girl.

"Nobody protected the two girls who got murdered last month."

The black woman's eyes flickered. Bess considered herself an excellent judge of emotion, and she saw grief, regret and sorrow before the eyes hardened again. "You a cop?"

Bess's mouth fell open before she laughed. That was a good one, she thought. Sort of flattering. "No, I'm not a cop. I'm just trying to make a living. Did you know either of them? The women who were killed?"

"We don't like questions around here." The woman tilted her head. "If you're trying to make a living, let's see you do it."

Bess felt a quick ripple of unease. Not only was the woman gorgeous, she was big. Big and suspicious. Both qualities were going to make it difficult for Bess to hang back on the fringes and observe. But she considered herself an agile thinker and a quick study. After all, she reminded herself, she'd come here tonight to do business.

"Sure." Turning, she strutted slowly along the sidewalk. Her hips—and she didn't for a minute believe that her butt was skinny—swayed seductively.

Maybe her throat was a little dry. Maybe her heart was pounding a bit too quickly. But Bess McNee took a great deal of pride in her work.

She spotted the two men half a block away and licked her lips. The one on the left, the dark one, looked very promising.

* * *

"Look, rookie, the idea's to take one, maybe two." Alex scanned the sidewalk ahead. Hookers, drunks, junkies and those unfortunate enough to have to pass through them to get home. "My snitch says that the tall black one—Rosalie—knew both the victims."

"So why don't we just pick her up and take her in for questioning?" Judd Malloy was anxious for action. His detective's shield was only forty-eight hours old. And he was working with Alexi Stanislaski, a cop who had a reputation for moving quickly and getting the job done. "Better yet, why don't we go roust her pimp?"

Rookies, Alex thought. Why were they always teaming him up with rookies? "Because we want her cooperation. We're going to pick her up, book her for solicitation. Then we're going to talk to her, real nice, before Bobby can come along and tell her to clam up."

"If my wife finds out I spent the night picking up hookers—"

"A smart cop doesn't tell his family anything they'd don't need to know. And they don't need to know much." Alex's dark brown eyes were cool, very cool, as they flicked over his new partner's face. "Stanislaski's rule number one."

He spotted the blonde. She was staring at him. Alex stared back. Odd face, he thought. Sharp, sexy, despite the makeup she'd troweled on. Beneath all the gunk, her eyes were a vivid green. The face itself was all angles, some of them wrong. Her nose was slightly crooked, as if it had been broken. Some john or pimp, he figured, then skimmed his eyes down to her mouth.

Full, overfull, and a glossy red. It didn't please him at all that he felt a reaction to it. Not knowing what she was, what she did. Her chin came to a slight point, and with her prominent cheekbones it gave her face a triangular, foxlike look.

The clinging tube top and spandex capri pants showed every inch of her curvy, athletic little body. He'd always been a sucker for the athletic type—but he reminded himself just where this particular number got her exercise.

In any case, she wasn't the one he was looking for.

Now or never, Bess told herself, feeling her new acquaintance's eyes on her.

"Hey, baby..." Though she hadn't smoked since she'd been fifteen, her voice was husky. Saying a prayer to whatever gods were listening, she veered in on Alex. "Want to party?"

"Maybe." He hooked a finger in the top of her tube, and was surprised when she flinched. "You're not quite what I had it mind, sweetie."

"Oh?" What next? Combining instinct with her observations, she tossed her head and leaned into him. She had the quick impression of pressing against steel—hard, unyielding and very cool. "Just what *did* you have in mind?"

Then, for a moment, she had nothing at all on hers. Not with the way those dark eyes cut into her, through her. His knuckles were brushing her skin, just above the breasts. She felt the heat from them, from him. As she continued to stare, she was struck by a vivid image of the two of them, rolling on a narrow bed in some dark room.

And it had nothing to do with business.

It was the first time Alex had ever seen a hooker blush. It threw him off, made him want to apologize for the fantasy that had just whipped through his brain. Then he remembered himself.

"Just a different type, babe."

In her heels, they were eye-to-eye. It made him want to rub off the powders and paints to see what was beneath.

"I can be a different type," Bess said, delighted with her inspired response.

"Hey, girlfriend." Rosalie strutted over and slipped a friendly arm around Bess's shoulders. "You're not going to be greedy and take both of these boys, are you?"

"I—"

Pay dirt, Alex thought, and shifted his attention to Rosalie. "You two a team?"

"We are tonight." She glanced from Alex to his partner. "How 'bout you two?"

Judd searched for his voice. He'd rather have been facing a gunman in an alley. And he simply couldn't put his hands on this big, beautiful woman, when a picture of his wife's trusting face was flashing in his head like a neon light.

"Sure." He let out a long breath and tried to emulate some of Alex's cocky confidence.

Rosalie threw back her head and laughed before she stepped forward, bumping bodies with Judd. He gave way instinctively as a dark red flush crept up his neck. "I believe you're new at this, honey. Why don't you let Rosalie show you the ropes?"

Because his partner seemed to have developed laryngitis, Alex took over. "How much?"

"Well..." Rosalie didn't bother to look over at Bess, who had gone dead pale. "Special rate tonight. You get both of us for a hundred. That's the first hour." She leaned down and whispered something in Judd's ear that had him babbling. "After that," she continued, "we can negotiate."

"I don't—" Bess began, then felt Rosalie's fingers dig into her bare shoulder like sharp little knives.

"I think that'll do it," Alex said, and pulled out his badge. "Ladies, you're busted."

Cops, Bess realized on a wave of sweet relief. While Rosalie expressed her opinion with a single vicious word, Bess struggled not to burst into wild laughter.

Perfect, Bess thought as she was bumped along into the squad room. She'd been arrested for solicitation, and life couldn't be better. Trying to take everything in at once, she grinned as she scanned the station house. She'd been in one before, of course. As she always said, she took her work seriously. But not in this precinct. Not downtown.

It was dirty—grimy, really, she decided, making mental notes and muttering to herself. Floors, walls, the barred windows. Everything had a nice, picturesque coat of crud.

It smelled, too. She took a deep breath so that she wouldn't forget the ripe stench of human sweat, bitter coffee and strong disinfectant.

And it was noisy. With every nerve on sensory alert, she separated the din into ringing phones, angry curses, weeping, and the clickety-clack of keyboards at work.

Man, oh, man, she thought. Her luck was really in.

"You're not a tourist, sweetheart," Alex reminded her, adding a firm nudge.

"Sorry."

The vibrant excitement in her eyes was so out of place that he stared. Then, with a shake of his head, he jabbed a finger toward a chair. He was letting the rookie get his feet wet getting the vitals from Rosalie. Once they had her booked, he'd take over himself, using charm or threats or whatever seemed most expedient to make her talk to him about her two murdered associates.

"Okay." He took his seat behind his battered and overcrowded desk. "You know the drill."

She'd been staring at a young man of about twenty with a face full of bruises and a torn denim jacket. "Excuse me?"

Alex just sighed as he rolled a form onto his typewriter. "Name?"

"Oh, I'm Bess." She held out her hand in a gesture so natural and friendly he nearly took it.

Instead, he swore softly. "Bess what?"

"McNee. And you're?"

"In charge. Date of birth."

"Why?"

His eyes flicked up, arrowed hers. "Why what?"

"Why do you want to know?"

Patience, never his strong suit, strained. He tapped a finger on the form. "Because I've got this space to fill."

"Okay. I'm twenty-eight. A Gemini. I was born on June the first."

Alex did the math and typed in the year. "Residence."

Natural curiosity had her poking through the folders and papers on his desk until he slapped her hand. "You're awfully tense," she commented. "Is it because you work undercover?"

Damn that smile, he thought. It was sassy, sexy, and far from stupid. That, and those sharp, intelligent green eyes, might have fooled him. But she looked like a hooker, and she smelled like a hooker. Therefore . . .

"Listen, doll, here's the way this works. I ask the questions, you answer them."

"Tough, cynical, street-smart."

One dark brow lifted. "Excuse me?"

"Just a quick personality check. You want my address, right?" she rattled off an address that made both of Alex's brows raise.

"Let's get serious."

"Okay." Willing to oblige, Bess folded her hands on the edge of his desk.

"Your address," he repeated.

"I just gave it to you."

"I know what real estate goes for in that area. Maybe you're good." Thoughtful, he scanned her attributes one more time. "Maybe you're better than you look. But you don't make enough working the streets to pop for that kind of rent."

Bess knew an insult when it hit her over the head. What made it worse was that she'd spent over an hour on her makeup. And she happened to know that her body was good. Lord knew, she sweated to keep it that way by working out three days a week. "That's where I live, cop." Her temper, which had a habit of flaring quickly, had her upending her enormous canvas tote onto his desk.

Alex watched, fascinated, as she pawed through the pile of contents. There were enough cosmetics to supply a small department store. And they weren't the cheap kind. Six lipsticks, two compacts, several mascara sticks and pots of eye shadow. A rainbow of eyeliner pencils. Scattered with them were two sets of keys, a snowfall of credit-card receipts, rubber bands, paper clips, twelve pens—he counted—a few broken pencils, a steno pad, two paperback books, matches, a leather address book embossed with the initials *ELM,* a stapler—he didn't even pause to wonder why she would carry one—tissues and crumpled papers, a tiny micro-cassette recorder. And a gun.

He whipped it out of the pile and stared at it. A water gun.

"Careful with that," she warned as she found her overburdened wallet. "It's full of ammonia."

"Ammonia?"

"I used to carry Mace, but this works fine. Here." Pleased with herself, she pushed the open wallet under his nose.

It might have been her in the picture. The hair was short and curly and chic, a deep chestnut rather than a brassy blonde. But that nose, that chin. And those eyes. He frowned over the driver's license. The address was right.

"You got a car?"

She shrugged and began to dump things back into her purse. "So?"

"Women in your position usually don't."

Because it made sense, Bess stalled. "I've got a license. Everybody who has a license doesn't have to have a car, do they?"

"No." He jerked the wallet out of her reach. "Take off the wig."

Pouting a little, she patted it. "How come?"

He reached across the desk and yanked it off himself. She scowled at him while she ran her fingers through short, springy red curls. "I want that back. It's borrowed."

"Sure." He tossed it onto his desk before he leaned back in his squeaky chair for a fresh evaluation. If this lady was a hooker, he was Clark Kent. "What the hell *are* you?"

It was time to come clean. She knew it. But something about him egged her on. "I'm just a woman trying to make a living, Officer." That was how Jade would handle it, Bess was sure. And since Jade was her creation, Bess was determined to do right by her.

He opened the wallet, skimmed through the bills. She was carrying around what would be for him more than two weeks' pay. "Right."

"Can you do that?" she demanded, more curious than annoyed. "Go through my personal property?"

"Honey, right now *you* are *my* personal property." There were pictures in the wallet, as well. Snapshots of people, some with her, some without her. And the lady was a card-carrying member of dozens of groups, including Greenpeace, the World Wildlife Federation, Amnesty International and the Writers' Guild. The last brought him back to the tape recorder. When he picked up the little toy, he noted that it was running. "Let's have it, Bess."

God, he was cute. The thought passed through her head as she smiled at him. "Have what?"

"What were you doing hanging around with Rosalie and the rest of the girls?"

"My job." When his eyes narrowed that way, Bess thought, he was downright irresistible. Impatient, a little mean, with a flash of recklessness just barely under control.

Fabulous.

"Really." All honesty and cheap perfume, she leaned forward. "You see, it all has to do with Jade, and how she's having this problem with a dual personality. By day, she's a dedicated lawyer—a real straight arrow, *you* know—but by night she hits the streets. She's blocking what happened between her and Brock, and coupled with a childhood memory that's begun to resurface, the strain's been too much for her. She's on a path of self-destruction."

The frown in his eyes turned them nearly black. "Who the hell is Jade?"

"Jade Sullivan Carstairs. Don't you watch daytime TV?"

His head was beginning to buzz. "No."

"You don't know what you're missing. You'd probably really enjoy the Jade-Storm-Brock story line. Storm's a cop, you see, and he's falling in love with Jade. Her emotional problems, and the hold Brock has on her, complicate things. Then there was a miscarriage, and the kidnapping. Naturally, Storm has problems of his own."

"Naturally. What's your point?"

"Oh, sorry. I get offtrack. I write for 'Secret Sins' Daytime drama."

"You're a soap-opera writer?"

"Yeah." Unlike many in the trade, she wasn't bothered by that particular label. "And I like to get the feel of the situations I put my characters into. Since Jade is a special pet of mine, I—"

"Are you out of your mind?" Alex barked the question as he leaned over into her face. "Do you have any idea what you were doing?"

She blinked, at once innocent and amused. "Research?"

He swore again, and Bess found she liked the way he raked impatient fingers through his thick black hair. "Lady, just how far were you intending to take your research?"

"How—? Oh." Her eyes brightened with laughter. "Well no, not quite that far."

"What the hell would you have done if I hadn't been a cop?"

"I'd have thought of something." She continued to smile. He had a fascinating face—golden skin, dark eyes, wonderful bones. And that mouth, so beautifully sculpted, even if it did tend to scowl. "It's my job to think of things. And when I spotted you, I thought you looked safe. What I mean is, you didn't strike me as the kind of man who'd be interested in . . ." What was a delicate way of putting it? she wondered. "Paying for pleasure."

He was so angry he wanted to yank her up and toss her over his lap. The idea of administering a few good whacks to that cute little butt was tremendously appealing. "And if you'd guessed wrong?"

"I didn't," she pointed out. "For a minute there, I was worried, but it all worked out. Better than I expected, really, because I had a chance to ride in a— Do you still call them paddy wagons?"

He'd been so sure he'd seen everything. Heard everything. With his temper straining at the bit, he spoke through clenched teeth. "Two hookers are dead. Two who worked that area."

"I know," she said quickly, as if that explained it all. "That was one of the reasons I chose it. You see, I plan to have Jade—"

"I'm talking about you," he interrupted in a voice that had her wincing. "You. Some bubbleheaded hack writer who thinks she can strut around in spandex and a half a ton of makeup, then go home to her nice neighborhood and wash it all off."

"Hack?" It was the only thing she took offense to. "Look, cop—"

"*You* look. You stay out of my territory, and out of those slut clothes. Do your research out of a book."

Her chin shot out. "I can go where I want, wearing what I want."

"You think so?" There was a way to teach her a lesson. A perfect way. "Fine." He rose, tugged the tote out of her hands, then took a firm grip on her arm. "Let's go."

"Where?"

"To holding, babe. You're under arrest, remember?"

She stumbled in the three-inch heels and squawked, "But I just explained—"

"I hear better stories before breakfast every day."

"You're not going to put me in a cell." Bess was sure of it. Positive. Right up until the moment the bars closed in her face.

It took about ten minutes for the shock to wear off. When it did, Bess decided it wasn't such a bad turn. She could be furious with the cop—whoever he was— but she could appreciate and take advantage of the unique opportunity he'd given her. She was in a holding cell with several other women. There was atmosphere to be absorbed, and there were interviews to be conducted.

When one of her cellmates informed her that she was entitled to a phone call, she demanded one. Pleased with the progress she was making, she settled back on her hard cot to talk to her new acquaintances.

It was thirty minutes later when she looked up and spotted her friend and cowriter Lori Banes, standing beside a uniformed policeman.

"Bess, you look so natural here."

With a grin, Bess popped up as the guard unlocked the door. "It's been great."

"Hey!" one of her cellmates called out. "I'm telling you that Vicki's a witch, and Jeffrey should boot her out. Amelia's the right woman for him."

Bess sent back a wink. "I'll see what I can do. 'Bye, girls."

Lori didn't consider herself long-suffering. She didn't consider herself a prude or a stuffed shirt. And she said as much to Bess as they walked through the corridors, up the stairs and back into the lobby area outside the squad room. "But," she added, pressing fingers to her tired eyes. "There's something that puts me off about being woken up at 2:00 a.m. to come bail you out of jail."

"Sorry, but it's been great. Wait until I tell you."

"Do you know what you look like, dear?"

"Yep." Unconcerned, Bess craned her neck. The chair behind Alex's desk was empty. "I had no idea that so many of the working girls watched the show. But they do work nights, mostly. Uh, excuse me..." She caught the sleeve of one of New York's finest as he walked by. "The officer who uses that desk?"

The cop swallowed the best part of a bite of his pastrami sandwich. "Stanislaski?"

"Whew. That's a mouthful. Is he still around?"

"He's in Interrogation."

"Oh. Thanks."

"Come on, Bess, we've got to pick up your things."

Bess had signed for her purse and its contents, still keeping an eye out for Alex. "Stanislaski," she repeated to herself. "Is that Polish, do you think?"

"How the hell do I know?" Out of patience, Lori steered her toward the door. "Let's get out of here. The place is lousy with criminals."

"I know. It's fabulous." With a laugh, she tucked an arm around Lori's waist. "I got ideas for the next three years. If we decide to have Elana arrested for Reed's murder..."

"I don't know about having Reed murdered."

With a sigh, Bess looked around for a cab. "Lori, we both know Jim isn't going to sign another contract. He wants to try the big leagues. Having his character offed is the perfect way to beef up Elana's story line."

"Maybe."

Bess slyly pulled out her ace. "'Our Lives, Our Loves' picked up two points in the ratings last month."

Lori only grunted.

"Word is Dr. Amanda Jamison is going to have twins."

"Twins?" Lori shut her eyes. Soap diva Ariel Kirkwood, who played the long-suffering psychiatrist on the competing soap, was daytime's most popular star. "It had to be twins," Lori muttered. "Okay, Reed dies."

Bess allowed herself one quick victory smile, then hurried on.

"Anyway, while I was in there, I was picturing the elegant, cool Dr. Elana Warfield Stafford Carstairs in prison. Fabulous, Lori. It'd be fabulous. I wish you'd seen the cop."

They'd walked to the corner, and there wasn't a cab in sight. "What cop?"

"The one who arrested me. He was incredibly sexy."

Lori only had the energy to sigh. "Leave it to you to get busted by a sexy cop."

"Really. All this thick black hair. His eyes were nearly black, too. Very intense. He had all those hollows and planes in his face, and this beautiful mouth. Nice build, too. Sort of rough-and-ready. Like a boxer, maybe."

"Don't start, Bess."

"I'm not. I can find a man sexy and attractive without falling in love."

Lori shot her a look. "Since when?"

"Since the last time. I've sworn off, remember?" Her smile perked up when she spotted a cab heading their way. "I'm interested in this Stanislaski for strictly professional reasons."

"Right." Resigned, Lori climbed in when the cab swung to the curb.

"I swear." She lifted her right hand to add impact to the oath. "We want to get into Storm's head more, into his background and stuff. So I pick this cop's brain a little." She gave a cabbie both her address and Lori's. "After Jade gets attacked by the Millbrook Maniac, Storm isn't going to be able to hold back his feelings for her. More has to come out about who and what he is. If we do have Elana arrested for Reed's murder, that's going to complicate his life—you know, family loyalty versus professional ethics. And once he confronts Brock—"

"Hey." At a red light, the cabbie turned, peering at them from under his fading Mets cap. "You talking about 'Secret Sins'?"

"Yeah." Bess brightened. "Do you watch it?"

"The wife tapes it every day. You don't look familiar."

"We're not on it," Bess explained. "We write it."

"Gotcha." Satisfied, he punched the accelerator when the light changed. "Let me tell you what I think about that two-timing Vicki."

As he proceeded to do just that, Bess leaned forward, debating with him. Lori closed her eyes and tried to catch up on lost sleep.

Chapter Two

"My wife went nuts." Judd Malloy munched on his cherry Danish while Alex swung in and out of downtown traffic. "She's a big fan of that soap, you know? Tapes it every day when she's in school."

"Terrific." Alex had been doing his best to forget his little encounter with the soap queen, but his partner wasn't cooperating.

"Holly figures it was just like meeting a celebrity."

"You don't find many celebrities turning tricks."

"Come on, Alex." Judd washed down the Danish with heavily sugared coffee. "She wasn't, really. You said so yourself, or the charges wouldn't have been dropped."

"She was stupid," Alex said between his teeth. "Carrying a damn water pistol in that suitcase of hers. I guess she figured if a john got rough, she'd blat him between the eyes and that would be that."

Judd started to comment on how it might feel to get a blat of ammonia in the eyes, but didn't think his partner wanted to hear it. "Well, Holly was impressed, and we got some fresh juice out of Rosalie, so we didn't waste our time."

"Malloy, you'd better get used to wasting time. Stanislaski's rule number four." Alex spotted the building he was looking for and double-parked. He was already out of the car and across the sidewalk before Judd found the NYPD sign and stuck it in the window. "We sure as hell could be wasting it here with this Domingo."

"Rosalie said—"

"Rosalie said what we wanted to hear so we'd spring her," Alex told him. His cop's eyes were already studying the building, noting windows, fire escapes, roof. "Maybe she gave us the straight shot on Domingo, and maybe she pulled it out of a hat. We'll see."

The place was in good repair. No graffiti, no broken glass or debris. Lower-middle-income, Alex surmised. Established families, mostly blue-collar. He pulled open the heavy entrance door, then scanned the names above the line of mailboxes.

"J. Domingo. 212." Alex pushed the buzzer for 110, waited, then hit 305. The answering buzz released the inner door. "People are so careless," he commented. He could feel Judd's nerves shimmering as they climbed the stairs, but he could tell he was holding it together. He'd damn well better hold it together, Alex thought as he gestured Judd into position, then knocked on the door of 212. He knocked a second time before he heard the cursing answer.

When the door opened a crack, Alex braced his body against it to keep it that way. "How's it going, Jesus?"

"What the hell do you want?"

He fit Rosalie's description, Alex noted. Right down to the natty Clark Gable moustache and the gold incisor. "Conversation, Jesus. Just a little conversation."

"I don't talk to nobody at this hour."

When he tried to shove the door to, Alex merely leaned on it and flipped open his badge. "You don't want to be rude, do you? Why don't you ask us in?"

Swearing in Spanish, Jesús Domingo cracked the door a little wider. "You got a warrant?"

"I can get one, if you want more than conversation. I can take you down for questioning, get the paperwork and do the job before your shyster lawyer can tap-dance you out. Want a team of badges in here, Jesus?"

"I haven't done nothing." He stepped back from the door, a small man with wiry muscles who was wearing nothing but a pair of gym shorts.

"Nobody said you did. Did I say he did, Malloy?"

Enjoying himself, Judd stepped in behind Alex. "Nope."

The building might be lower-middle-class, but Domingo's apartment was a small high-tech palace. State-of-the-art stereo equipment, Alex noted. A big-screen TV with some very classy video toys. The wall of tapes ran mostly to the X-rated.

"Nice place," Alex commented. "You sure know how to make your unemployment check stretch."

"I got a good head for figures." Domingo plucked up a pack of cigarettes from a table, lighted one. "So?"

"So, let's talk about Angie Horowitz."

Domingo blew out smoke and scratched at the hair on his chest. "Never heard of her."

"Funny, we got word you were one of her regulars, and her main supplier."

"You got the wrong word."

"Maybe you don't recognize the name." Alex reached into his inside jacket pocket, and his fingers brushed over his leather shoulder harness as he pulled out a manila envelope. "Why don't you take a look?" He stuck the police shot under Domingo's nose and watched his olive complexion go a sickly gray. "Look familiar?"

"Man." Domingo's fingers shook as he brought his cigarette to his lips.

"Problem?" Alex glanced down at the photo himself. There hadn't been much left of Angie for the camera. "Oh, hey, sorry about that, Jesus. Malloy, didn't I tell you not to put the dead shot in?"

Judd shrugged, feigning casualness. He was thinking he was glad he didn't have to look at it again himself. "Guess I made a mistake."

"Yeah." All the while he spoke, Alex held the photo where Domingo could see it. "Guy's a rookie," he explained. "Always screwing up. You know. Poor little Angie sure got sliced, didn't she? Coroner said the guy put about forty holes in her. You can see most of them. Poor Malloy here took one look and lost his breakfast. I keep telling him not to eat those damned greasy Danishes before we go check out a stiff, but like

I said . . ." Alex grinned to himself as Domingo made a dash for the bathroom.

"That was cold, Stanislaski," Judd said, grinning.

"Yeah, I'm that kind of guy."

"And I didn't throw up my breakfast."

"You wanted to." The sounds coming from the bathroom were as unpleasant as they get. Alex tapped on the door. "Hey, Jesús, you okay, man? I'm really sorry about that." He passed the photo and envelope to Judd. "Tell you what, let me get you some nice cold water, okay?"

The answer was a muffled retch that Alex figured anyone could take for assent. He moved into the kitchen and opened the freezer. The two kilos were exactly where Rosalie had said he'd find them. He took one out just as Domingo rushed in.

"You got no warrant. You got no right."

"I was getting you some ice." Alex turned the frozen cocaine over in his hands. "This doesn't look like a TV dinner to me. What do you think, Malloy?"

By leaning a shoulder against the door jamb, Judd blocked the doorway. "Not the kind my mother used to make."

"You son of a bitch." Domingo wiped his mouth with a clenched fist. "You violated my civil rights. I'll be out before you can blink."

"Could be." Taking an evidence bag out of his pocket, Alex slipped both kilos inside. "Malloy, why don't you read our friend his rights while he's getting dressed? And, Jesús, try some mouthwash."

"Stanislaski," the desk sergeant called out when Alex came up from seeing Domingo into a cell. "You got company."

Alex glanced over toward his desk, seeing that several cops were huddled around it. There was quite a bit of laughter overriding the usual squad room noise. Curiosity had him moving forward even before he saw the legs. Legs he recognized. They were crossed at the knee and covered almost modestly in a canary-yellow skirt.

He recognized the rest of her, too, though the tough little body was clad in a multihued striped blazer and a scoop-necked blouse the same color as the skirt. Half a dozen slim columns of gold danced at her ears as she laughed. She looked better, sexier, he was forced to admit, with her mouth unpainted, her freckles showing, and those big green eyes subtly smudged with color. Her hair was artfully tousled, a rich, deep red that made him think of a mahogany statue his brother had carved for him.

"So I told the mayor we'd try to work it in, and we'd love for him to come on the show and do a cameo." She shifted on the desk and spotted Alex. He was frowning at her, his thumbs tucked into the pockets of a leather bomber jacket. "Officer Stanislaski."

"McNee." He inclined his head, then swept his gaze over his fellow officers. "The boss comes in and finds you here, I might have to tell him how you didn't have enough work and volunteered to take some of mine."

"Just entertaining your guest, Stanislaski." But the use of the squad room's nickname for their captain had the men drifting reluctantly away.

"What can I do for you?"

"Well, I—"

"You're sitting on a homicide," he told her.

"Oh." She scooted off the desk. Without the stilettos, she was half a head shorter than he. Alex discovered he preferred it that way. "Sorry. I came by to thank you for straightening things out for me."

"That's what they pay me for. Straightening things out." He'd been certain she would rave a bit about being tossed into a cell, but she was smiling, friendly as a kindergarten teacher. Though he couldn't recall ever having a teacher who looked like her. Or smelled like her.

"Regardless, I appreciate it. My producer's very tolerant, but if it had gone much further, she would have been annoyed."

"Annoyed?" Alex repeated. He stripped off his jacket and tossed it onto his chair. "She'd have been annoyed to find out that one of her writers was out soliciting johns down at Twenty-third and Eleventh Avenue."

"Researching," Bess corrected, unoffended. "Darla—that's my producer—she gets these headaches. I gave her a whopper when I went on a job with a cat burglar."

"With a..." He let his words trail off and eased down on the spot on the desk she'd just vacated. "I don't think you want to tell me about that."

"Actually, he was a former cat burglar. Fascinating guy. I just had him show me how he'd break into my apartment." She frowned a little, remembering. "I guess he was a little rusty. The alarm—"

"Don't." Alex held up a hand. He was beginning to feel a headache coming on himself.

"That's old news, anyway." She waved it away with a cheerful gesture of her hands. "Do you have a first name, or do I just call you Officer?"

"It's Detective."

"Your first name is Detective?"

"No, my rank." He let out a sigh. "Alex."

"Alex. That's nice." She ran a fingertip over the strap of his harness. She wasn't being provocative; she wanted to know what it felt like. Once she knew him better, she was sure, she'd talk him into letting her try it on. "Well, Alex, I was wondering if you'd let me use you."

He'd been a cop for more than five years, and until this moment he hadn't thought anything could surprise him. But it took him three seconds to close his mouth. "I beg your pardon?"

"It's just that you're so perfect." She stepped closer. She really wanted to get a better look at his weapon—without being obvious about it.

She smelled like sunshine and sex. As he drew it in, Alex thought that combination would baffle any man. "I'm perfect?"

"Absolutely." She looked straight into his eyes and smiled. Her gaze was frank and assessing. She was studying him, the way a woman might study a dress in a showroom window. "You're exactly what I've been looking for."

Her eyes were pure green. No hint of gray or blue, no flecks of gold. There was a small dimple near her mouth. Only one. Nothing about that odd, sexy face was balanced. "What you're looking for?"

"I know you're busy, but I'd try not to take up too much of your time. An hour now and then."

"An hour?" He caught himself echoing her, and shook himself loose. "Listen, I appreciate—"

"You're not married, are you?"

"Married? No, but—"

"That makes it simpler. It just came to me last night when I was getting into bed."

God. He'd learned to appreciate women early. And he'd learned to juggle them skillfully—if he said so himself. He knew how to dodge, when to evade and when to sit back and enjoy. But with this one, all bets were off.

"Is this heavy?" she asked, fiddling with his harness.

"You get used to it. It's just there."

Her smile warmed, making him think of sunlight again. "Perfect," she murmured. "I'd be willing to compensate you for your time, and your expertise."

"You'd be—" He wasn't certain if he was insulted or embarrassed. "Hold on, babe."

"Just think about it," Bess said quickly. "I know it's a lot to ask, but I have this problem with Matthew."

A brand-new emotion snuck in under his guard, and it was as green as her eyes. "Matthew? Who the hell is Matthew?"

"We call him Storm, actually. Lieutenant Storm Warfield, Millbrook PD."

Now he definitely had a headache. Alex rubbed his fingers against his temple. "Millbrook?"

"The fictional town of Millbrook, where the show's set. It's supposed to be somewhere in the Midwest. Storm's a cop. Personally, his life's a mess, but professionally, he's focused and intense and occasionally ruthless. In this new story line I'm working on, I want to concentrate on his police work, the routine, the frustrations."

"Wait." He'd always been quick, but it was taking him a minute to change gears. "You want me to help you with a story line?"

"Exactly. If you could just tell me how you think, how you go about solving a case, working with the system or around it. TV cops have to work around the system quite a bit, you know. It plays better than by-the-book."

He swore under his breath and rubbed his hands over his face. Damn it, his palms were sweaty. "You're a real case, McNee."

"You don't have to decide right now." She was also persistent. And she wondered if he had a spare gun strapped to his calf. One of those sexy-looking little chrome jobs. She'd seen that ploy in several movies. Still, she thought if she asked him that, she'd lose her edge. "I'm having a thing tonight." As she spoke, she dug into her huge bag for her notebook. "Eight o'clock until whenever. Bring a friend, if you like. Your partner, too. He seemed very sweet."

"He's adorable."

"Yeah." She ripped off the page and handed it to him. "I'd really like you to stop by."

He took the sheet, not bothering to remind her he already had her address. "Why?"

"Why not?" She beamed at him again.

Before he could list the reasons, he heard his name called.

"Alexi."

Alexi. Bess was already enchanted with the sound as she rolled the name over in her head. Different, exotic. Sexy. She was certain it suited him much more than the casual *Alex.*

Bess studied the woman bearing down on them. This wasn't one who'd be lost in a crowd, she mused. She was stunning, totally self-assured and very pregnant. Beside Bess, Alex pushed off the desk and sighed.

"Rachel."

"A moment of your time, Detective," Rachel said, flipping a glance over Bess before pinning Alex with a tawny stare. "To reacquaint you with civil rights."

"Your sister?" Bess surmised, beaming at both of them.

Alex sent her a considering frown. "How did you know that?"

"I'm really good with faces. Same bone structure, same coloring, same mouth. You have to be brother and sister, or first cousins."

"Guilty," Rachel admitted. Though she would have liked to know what Alex was doing with the sharp-eyed redhead, she wasn't about to be swayed from her duties as a public defender. "Jesús Domingo, Alexi. Illegal search and seizure."

"Bull." Alex crossed his arms and leaned back against the desk.

"You had a search warrant?"

"Didn't need one. He invited us in."

"And invited you to poke through his belongings, I suppose."

"Nope." Alex grinned while Bess watched them bounce the verbal ball as though they were champion tennis players. "Jesús got sick. I offered to get him some water. He didn't object. I opened the freezer to get the poor guy some ice, and there it was. Two kilos. It'll all be in my report."

"That's lame, Alexi. You'll never get a conviction."

"Maybe. Maybe not. Talk to the DA."

"I intend to." Rachel shifted her briefcase and began to rub her belly in circular motions to soothe the baby, who seemed to be doing aerobics in her womb. "You had no probable cause."

"Sit down."

"I don't want to sit down."

"The baby does." He yanked over a chair and all but shoved her into it. "When are you going to knock this off?"

It did feel better to sit. Indescribably better. But she wasn't about to admit it. "The baby's not due for two months. I have plenty of time. We were discussing . . ."

"Rach." He laid a hand on her cheek, very gently. A shouted curse wouldn't have stopped her, but the small gesture did. "Don't make me worry about you."

"I'm perfectly fine."

"You shouldn't be here."

"I'm having a baby. It's not contagious. Now, about Domingo."

Alex gave a brief, pithy opinion on what could be done with Domingo. "Talk to the DA," he repeated. "Sitting down."

"She looks pretty strong to me," Bess commented. Two pair of eyes turned to her, one furious, the other thoughtful.

"Thank you. The men in my life are coddlers," Rachel explained. "Sweet, but annoying."

"Muldoon should take better care of you," Alex insisted.

"I don't need Zack to take care of me. And the fact is, between him and Nick, I'm barely allowed to brush my own teeth." She held out a hand to Bess. "Since my brother is too rude to introduce me, I'm Rachel Muldoon."

"Bess McNee. You're a lawyer?"

"That's right. I work for the public defender's office."

"Really?" Bess's thoughts began to perk. "What's it like to—"

Alex held up a hand. "Don't get her started. She'll pick your brain clean before you know she's had her fingers in it. Look, McNee—" he turned to Bess, determined not to be charmed by her easy smile "—we're a little busy here."

"Of course you are. I'm sorry." Obligingly she swung her huge purse onto her shoulder. "We'll talk tonight. Nice to meet you, Rachel."

"Same here." Rachel ran her tongue over her teeth, and both she and Alex watched Bess weave her way out of the squad room. "Well, that was rude."

"It's the only way to handle her. Believe me."

"Hmm... She seems like an interesting woman. How did you meet her?"

"Don't ask." He sat back down on his desk, irked that the scent of sunshine and sex still lingered in the air.

"I can't believe we're doing this." Holly, Judd's pretty wife of eight months, was all but hopping out of her party shoes. "Wait until I tell everyone in the teachers' lounge where I spent the evening."

"Take it easy, honey." Judd tugged at the tie she'd insisted he wear. "It's just a party."

"Just a party?" As the elevator rode up, she fussed with her honey-brown hair. "I don't know about you two, but it isn't every day I get to eat canapés with celebrities."

Ominously silent, Alex stayed hunched in his leather jacket. He didn't know what the hell he was doing here. His first mistake had been mentioning the invitation to Judd. No matter how insouciant Judd pretended to be, he'd been bursting at the seams when he called his wife. Alex had been swept along in their enthusiasm.

But he wasn't going to stay. Holly's sense of decorum might have insisted that she and Judd couldn't attend without him, but he'd already decided just how he'd play it. He'd go in, maybe have a beer and a couple of crackers. Then he'd slip out again. He'd be damned if he'd spend this rare free evening playing soap-opera groupie.

"Oh, my" was all Holly could say when the elevator doors opened.

The walls of the private foyer were splashed with a mural of the city. Times Square, Rockefeller Center, Harlem, Little Italy, Broadway. People seemed to be rushing along the walls, just as they did the streets below. It was as if the woman who lived here didn't want to miss one moment of the action.

The wide door to the main apartment was open, and music, laughter and conversation were pouring out, along with the scents of hot food and burning candles.

"Oh, my," Holly said again, dragging her husband along as she stepped inside.

From behind them, Alex scanned the room. It was huge, and it was packed with people. Draped in silk or cotton, clad in business suits and lush gowns, they stood elbow to elbow on the hardwood floor, lounged hip to hip on the sapphire cushions of the enormous circular conversation pit, sat knee to knee on the steps of a bronze circular staircase that led to an open loft where still more people leaned against a railing decked with naked cherubs.

Two huge windows let the lights of the city in. More partygoers sat on the pillow-plumped window seats, balancing plates and glasses on their laps.

Paintings were scattered over the ivory-toned walls. Vivid, frenetic modern art, mind-bending surrealism. There was enough color to make his head swim. Yet, through the crowd and the clashing tones, he saw her. Dancing seductively with a distinguished-looking man in a gray pin-striped suit.

She wore an excuse for a dress, the color of crushed purple grapes. He wondered, irritated, if she owned anything that covered those legs. This number certainly didn't. Nor did it cover much territory at all, the way it dipped to the waist in the back, skimmed above mid-thigh and left her shoulders bare, but for skinny, glittery straps. Multihued gemstones fell in a rope from her earlobes to those nicely sloped shoulders. Her feet were bare.

She looked, Alex thought as his stomach muscles twisted themselves into nasty knots, outrageously alluring.

"Oh, Lord, there's Jade. Oh, and Storm and Vicki. Dr. Carstairs, too." Holly's fingers dug into her husband's arm. "It's Amelia."

"Who?"

"'Secret Sins,' dummy." She gave Judd a playful punch. "The whole cast's here."

"That's not all." Because he remembered in time he was supposed to be jaded, Judd stopped himself from pointing and inclined his head. "That's Lawrence D. Strater dancing with our hostess. *The* L. D. Strater, of Strater Industries. The *Fortune* 500's darling. The mayor's over in that corner, talking with Hannah Loy, the grand old lady of Broadway." His excitement began to hum in his voice as he continued to scan the room. "Man, there are enough luminaries in this room to light every borough in New York."

But Alex hadn't noticed. Furthermore, he didn't give a damn. His attention was focused on Bess. She'd stopped dancing, and had leaned up to whisper something in her partner's ear that made him laugh before he kissed her. Smack on the lips.

She kissed him back, too, her hands lightly intimate at his waist, before she turned and spotted the new arrivals. She waved, made her excuses, then scooted and dodged her way through the crowd toward them.

"You made it." She gave both Alex and Judd a friendly peck on the cheek before holding out both hands to Holly. "Nice to meet you."

"My wife, Holly, this is Bess McNee."

"Thanks for asking us." Holly caught herself starting to stutter, as she had the first time she faced a classroom of ten-year-olds. She flushed.

"My pleasure." Bess gave her hands a reassuring squeeze. "Let's get you something to eat and drink." She gestured toward a long table by the wall. Instead of the useless finger food and fancy, unrecognizable dishes Alex had expected, it was laden with big pots of spaghetti, mountains of garlic bread, and generous trays of antipasti.

"It's Italian night," she explained, grabbing a plate and heaping it high. "There's plenty of wine and beer, and a full bar." She handed the plate to Holly and began to dish up another. "The desserts are on the other side of the room. They're unbelievable." As she passed Judd a plate, she noted the gleam in Holly's eyes. "Would you like to meet some of the cast?"

"Oh, I . . ." The hell with sophistication. "Yes. I'd love it."

"Great. Excuse us. Help yourself, Alexi."

"This is really something," Judd said over a mouthful of spaghetti.

"Something," Alex agreed. Deciding to make the best of it, he fixed himself a plate.

He wasn't going to stay. But the food was great. In any case, he didn't have anything else to do. It didn't hurt to hang around and rub elbows with the fast and famous while he was helping himself to a good hot meal. It certainly made a change from his daily routine of wading through misery and bitterness.

After washing down spaghetti with some good red wine, he found himself a spot on a window seat where he could sit back and watch the show.

Bess dropped down beside him, clinked her glass against his. "Best seat in the house."

"Some house."

"Yeah, I like it. I'll show you the rest later, if you want." She broke off a tiny piece of the pastry on his plate and sampled it. "Great stuff."

"Yeah. You got a little . . . here." Before his good sense could take over, he rubbed a bit of the rich cream from her lip. Watching her, he licked it from the pad of his thumb. And tasted her. "It's not bad."

For a moment she wondered if the circuits in her brain had crossed. Something certainly had sent out a spark. She managed a small sound of agreement as she flicked her tongue to the corner of her mouth. And tasted him.

"Your, ah, partner's wife. Holly." Small talk, any talk, had always come easily to her. She wasn't sure why she was laboring now.

"What about her?"

"Who? Oh, right. Holly. She's nice. I can't imagine what it would be like to teach fifth-graders."

"I'm sure you'll ask her."

"I already did." At ease again, she smiled at him. Something about that sarcastic edge to his voice made her relax and enjoy. "Come on, Alexi. We may be in different professions, but both of them require a certain amount of curiosity about human nature. Aren't you sitting here right now wondering about all of these people, and what they're doing at my party?"

"Not as much as I'm wondering what *I'm* doing at your party." He swirled the wine in his glass before sipping. When he drank, his eyes stayed on hers. Watchful.

She liked that. She liked that very much, the way he could sit so still, energy humming from every pore, while he watched. While he waited. Bess was willing to admit that one of her biggest failings was being unable to wait for anything.

"You were curious," she told him.

"Some."

Her skirt hitched up another inch when she curled her legs up on the seat. "I'd be happy to tell you whatever you want to know, in exchange for your help. You see that guy over there, the gorgeous one with the blonde hanging on his biceps?"

Alex scanned, homed in. "Yeah. I wouldn't say he was gorgeous."

"You're not a woman. That's my detective, Storm Warfield, the black sheep of the snooty, disgustingly rich Warfield clan, the rebel, the volatile brother of the long-suffering Elana Warfield Stafford Carstairs. He's recently pulled himself out of the destructive affair with the wicked, wily Vicki. The blonde crawling up his chest. They're an item off-camera, but on, Storm is madly in love with the tragedy-prone and ethereal Jade, who is, of course, torn between her feelings for him and her misplaced loyalty to the maniacally clever and dastardly Brock Carstairs—half brother to Elana's stalwart husband Dr. Maxwell Carstairs. Max was once married to Jade's formerly conniving but now repentant sister, Flame, who was killed in a Peruvian earthquake soon after the birth of her son— who may or may not be her husband's child. Naturally, the body was never recovered."

"Either I've had too much wine, or you're making me dizzy."

Bess smiled and gave him a companionable pat on the thigh that sent his blood pressure soaring. "It's really not that complicated, once you know the players. But I want you for Storm."

Alex sent the actor a considering look. "I don't think he's my type."

"Your professional expertise, Detective. I need an informal technical advisor. My producer'd be happy to compensate you for your time—particularly since we've been number one in the ratings for the past nine months." Someone called her name, and Bess sent a quick wave. "Looks like it's going to start to thin out. Listen, can you hang around until I've finished playing hostess?"

She popped up and was gone before he could answer. After a moment, Alex set the rest of the dessert aside and rose. If he was going to see the party through, he might as well enjoy himself.

As she saw to the rest of her guests, Bess kept an eye on him. Once he decided to relax, she noted, he made the most of it. It didn't surprise her that he knew how to flirt, or that several women in the room made a point of wandering in his direction. Not even Lori—no pushover in the men department—was unaffected.

"So, that's the one who busted you?" Lori asked her, popping a plump olive into her mouth.

"What do you think?"

Lori chewed, savored, swallowed. "Yum-yum."

With a laugh, Bess chose a wedge of cheese. "I assume that's a comment on the man, not my buffet."

"You bet. And the best part is, he's not an actor."

"Still sore?" Bess murmured.

Lori shrugged, but her gaze cut over to Steven Marshall, alias Brock Carstairs. "I never give him, or his weenie little brain, a thought. No sensible woman would spend her life competing with an actor's ego for attention."

"Sense has nothing to do with it."

Lori looked away, because it hurt, more than she could bear to admit, to watch Steven while he was so busy ignoring her. "This from the queen of the bungled relationships."

"I don't bungle them, I enjoy them."

"I hasten to remind you that two of your former fiancés are in this room."

"It's a big party. Besides, I wasn't engaged to Lawrence."

"He gave you a ring with a rock the size of a Buick."

"A token of his esteem," Bess said blithely. "I never agreed to marry him. And Charlie and I..." She waved to Charles Stutman, esteemed playwright. "We were only engaged for a few months. We both agreed Gabrielle was perfect for him and parted the closest of friends."

"It was the first time I'd heard of a woman being best man at her former fiancé's wedding," Lori admitted. "I don't know how you do it. You don't angst over men, and they never toss blame your way when things fall apart."

"Because I end up being a pal." Bess's lips curved. For the briefest of moments, there was something wistful in the smile. "Not always a position a woman craves, but it seems to suit me."

"Going to be pals with the cop?"

Once again Bess found herself searching the remaining guests for Alex. She found him, dancing slow and close with a sultry brunette. "It would help if he'd bring himself to like me a little. I think it's going to take some work."

"I've never known you to fail. I've got to go. See you Monday."

"Okay." Bess was astute enough to glance over in Steven's direction as Lori left. She was also clearsighted enough to see the expression of misery in his eyes as he watched Lori walk to the elevator.

People were much too hard on themselves, she thought with a sigh. Love, she was certain, was a complicated and painful process only if you wanted it to be. And she should know, she mused as she took another sip of wine. She had slipped painlessly in and out of love for years.

As she set the glass aside, Alex caught her eye. There was a quick, surprising tremor around her heart. But it was gone quickly as someone swept her up into a dance.

Chapter Three

"How often do you have one of these *things?*" Alex asked when he took Bess up on her offer of a last cup of cappuccino in her now empty and horribly cluttered apartment.

"Oh, when the mood strikes." The after-party wreckage didn't concern her. She and the cleaning team she'd hired would shovel it out sooner or later. Besides, she enjoyed this—the mess and debris, the spilled wine, the lingering scents. It was a testament to the fact that she, and a good many others, had enjoyed themselves.

"Want some cold spaghetti?" she asked him.

"No."

"I do." She unfolded herself from the corner section of the pit and wandered over to the buffet. "I didn't get a chance to eat much earlier—just what I could steal off other people's plates." She came back to stretch out on the cushions and twine pasta on her fork. "What did you think of Bonnie?"

"Who?"

"Bonnie. The brunette you were dancing with. The one who stuck her phone number in your pocket."

Remembering, Alex patted his shirt pocket. "Right. Bonnie. Very nice."

"Mmm...she is." As she agreed, Bess twined more pasta. She propped her feet on the coffee table, where they continued to keep the beat of the low-volume rock playing on the stereo. "I appreciate your staying."

"I've got some time."

"I still appreciate it. Let me run this by you, okay?" She continued to eat, rapidly working her way through a large plate full of food. "Jade's got a split personality due to an early-childhood trauma, which I won't go into."

"Thank God."

"Don't be snide—millions of viewers are panting for more. Anyway, Jade's alter ego, Josie, is the hooker—or will be, once we start taping that story line. Storm's nuts about Jade. It's difficult for him, as he's a very passionate sort of guy, and she's fragile at the moment."

"Because of Brock."

"You catch on. Anyway, he's wildly in love and miserably frustrated, and he's got a hot case to solve. The Millbrook Maniac."

"The—" Alex shut his eyes. "Oh, man."

"Hey, the press is always giving psychotics catchy little labels. Anyway, the Maniac's going around strangling women with a pink silk scarf. It's symbolic, but we won't get into that right now, either."

"I can't tell you how grateful I am."

She offered him a forkful of cold pasta. After a moment, he gave in and leaned closer to take it. "Now, the press is going to start hounding Storm," Bess continued. "And the brass will be on his case, too. His emotional life is a wreck. How does he separate it? How does he go about establishing a connection between the three—so far—victims? And when he realizes Jade may be in danger, how does he keep his personal feelings from clouding his professional judgement?"

"That's the kind of stuff you want?"

"For a start."

"Okay." He propped his feet beside hers. "First, you don't separate, not like you mean. The minute you have to think like a cop, that's what you are, that's how you think, and you've got no personal life until you can stop thinking like a cop again."

"Wait." Bess shoved the plate into his lap, then bounded up and hunted through a drawer until she came up with a notebook. She dropped onto the sofa again, curling up her legs this time, so that her knee lay against the side of his thigh. "Okay," she said, scribbling. "You're telling me that when you start on a case, or get a call or whatever, everything else just clicks off."

Since she seemed to be through eating, he set the plate on the coffee table. "It better click off."

"How?"

He shook his head. "There is no how. It just is. Look, cop work is mostly monotonous. It's routine, but it's the kind of routine you have to keep focused on. Make a mistake in the paperwork, and some slime gets bounced on a technicality."

"What about when you're on the street?"

"That's a routine, too, and you'd better keep your head on that routine, if you want to go home in one piece. You can't starting thinking about the fight you had with your woman, or the bills you can't pay, or the fact that your mother's sick. You think about now, right now, or you won't be able to fix any of those things later. You'll just be dead."

Her eyes flashed up to his. He said it so matter-of-factly. When she studied him, she saw that he thought of it that way. "What about fear?"

"You usually have about ten seconds to be afraid. So you take them."

"But what if the fear's for someone else? Someone you love?"

"Then you'd better put it aside and do what you've been trained to do. If you don't, you're no good to yourself or your partner, and you're a liability."

"So, it's cut-and-dried?"

He smiled a little. "Except on TV. You're asking me for feelings, McNee, intangibles."

"A cop's feelings," she told him. "I'd think they would be very tangible. Maybe a cop wouldn't be allowed to show his emotions on the job. An occasional flare-up, maybe, but then you'd have to suck it in and follow routine. And no matter how good you are, an arrest isn't always going to stick. The bad guy isn't always going to pay. That has to cause immeasurable frustration. And repressing that frustration . . ." Considering, she tapped her pencil against the pad. "See, I think of people as pressure cookers."

"Sure you do."

"No, really." That quick smile, the flash of the single dimple. "Whatever's inside, good or bad, has to have some means of release, or the lids blows." She shifted again, and her fingers nearly brushed his neck. She talked with them, he'd noted. With her hands, her eyes, her whole body. The woman simply didn't know how to be still. "What do you use to keep the lid on, Alexi?"

"I make sure I kick a couple of small dogs every morning."

She smiled with entirely too much understanding. "Too personal? Okay, we'll come back to it later."

"It's not personal." Damn it, she made him uncomfortable. As if he had an itch in the small of his back that he couldn't quite scratch. "I use the gym. Beat the crap out of a punching bag a few days a week. Lift too many weights. Sweat it out."

"That's great. Perfect." Grinning now, she cupped a hand over his biceps and squeezed. "Not too shabby. I guess it works." She flexed her own arm, inviting him to test the muscle. It was the gesture of a small boy on a playground, but Alex couldn't quite think of her that way. "I work out myself," she told him. "I'm addicted to it. But I can't seem to develop any upper-body strength."

He watched her eyes as he curled a hand over her arm and found a tough little muscle. "Your upper body looks fine."

"A compliment." Surprised that a reaction had leapt straight into her gut at the casual touch, she started to move her arm. He held on. It took some work to keep her smile from faltering. "What? You want to arm-wrestle, Detective?"

Her skin was like rose petals—smooth, fragrant. Experimenting, he skimmed his hand down to the curve of her elbow. She was smiling, he noted, and her eyes were lit with humor, but her pulse was racing. "A few years back I arm-wrestled my brother for his wife. I lost."

The idea was just absurd enough to catch her imagination. "Really? Is that how the Stanislaskis win their women?"

"Whatever works." Because he was tempted to explore more of that silky, exposed skin, he rose. He reminded himself that the uncomplicated Bonnie was more his style than the overinquisitive, oddly packaged Bess McNee. "I have to go."

Whatever had been humming between them was fading now. As Bess walked him to the door, she debated with herself whether she wanted to let those echoes fade or pump up the volume until she recognized the tune. "Stanislaski. Is that Polish, Russian, what?"

"We're Ukrainian."

"Ukrainian?" Intrigued, she watched him pull his jacket on. "From the southwest of the European Soviet Union, with the Carpathian Mountains in the west."

"Yeah." And through those mountains his family had escaped when he was no more than a baby. He felt a tug, a small one, as he often did when he thought of the country of his blood. "You've been there?"

"Only in spirit." Smiling, she straightened his jacket for him. "I minored in geography in college. I like reading about exotic places." She kept her hands on the front of his jacket, enjoying the feel of leather, the scent of it, and of him. Their bodies were close, more casual than intimate, but close. Looking into his eyes, those dark, uncannily focused eyes, she discovered she wanted to hear that tune again after all.

"Are you going to talk to me again?" she asked him.

His fingers itched to roam along that tantalizingly bare skin on her back. For reasons he couldn't have named, he kept his hands at his side. "You know where to find me. If I've got the time and the answers, we'll talk."

"Thanks." Her lips curved as she rose on her toes so that their eyes and mouths were level. She leaned in slowly, an inch, then two, to touch her mouth to his. The kiss was soft and breezy. Either of his sisters might have said goodbye to him in precisely the same manner. But that cool and fleeting taste of her didn't make him feel brotherly.

She heard the humming in her head. A nice, quiet sound of easy pleasure. He tasted faintly of wine and spices, and his firm lips seemed to accept the gesture as it was meant—as one of affection and curiosity. Her lips were still curved when she dropped back on her heels.

"Good night, Alexi."

He nodded. He was fairly sure he could speak, but there was no point in taking the chance. Turning, he walked into the foyer and punched the elevator button. When he glanced back, she was still standing in the doorway. Smiling, she waved another goodbye and started to close the door.

It surprised them both when he whirled around and slapped a hand on it to keep it open. The fact that she took an automatic step in retreat surprised her further. But it was the look in his eyes, she thought, that made her feel like a rabbit caught in a rifle's cross hairs.

"Did you forget something?"

"Yeah." Very slowly, very deliberately, he slid his arms around her waist, ran his hand up her back, so that her eyes widened and her skin shivered. "I forgot I like to make my own moves."

Bess braced for the kind of wild assault that was in his eyes, and was surprised for the third time in as many minutes. He didn't swoop or crush, but eased her closer, degree by degree, until she was molded to him. His fingers cruised lazily up her back until they reached the nape of her neck, where they cupped and held. Still his mouth hovered above her.

His hand moved low, intimately, where skin gave way to silk. "Stand on your toes," he murmured.

"What?"

"Stand on your toes." This time, it was his lips that curved.

Dazed, she obeyed, then gave a strangled gasp when he increased the pressure on her back and pressed them center to center. His eyes stayed open as he moved his mouth to hers, brushing, nipping, then taking, in a dreamy kind of possession that had her own vision blurring.

The humming in her brain increased until it was a wall of sound, unrecognizable. She was deaf to everything else, even her own throaty moan as he dipped his tongue between her lips to seduce hers.

It was all slow-motion and soft-focus, but that didn't stop the heat from building. She could feel the little flames start to flare where she was pressed most intimately against him, then spread long, patient fingers of fire outward. Everywhere.

He never pushed, he never pressured, he savored, as a man might who had enjoyed a satisfying meal and was content to linger over a tasty dessert. Even knowing she was being sampled, tested, lazily consumed, she couldn't protest. For the first time in her life, Bess understood what it was to be helplessly seduced.

He hadn't meant to do this. He'd been thinking about doing just this for hours. However much pleasure it gave him to feel her curvy body melt against his, to hear those small, vulnerable sounds vibrating in her throat, to taste that dizzy passion on her lips, he knew he'd made a mistake.

She wasn't his type. And he was going to want more.

The instinct he'd been born with and then honed during his years on the force helped him to hold back that part of himself that, if let loose, could turn the evening into a disaster for both of them. Still, he lingered another moment, taking himself to the edge. When his system was churning with her, and his mind was clouded with visions of peeling her out of that swatch of a dress, he stepped back. He supported her by the elbows until her eyes fluttered open.

They were big and dazed. He clenched his teeth to fight back the urge to pull her to him again and finish what he'd started. But, however stunned and fragile she looked at the moment, Alex recognized a dangerous woman. He'd been a cop long enough to know when to face danger, and when to avoid it.

"You, ah..." Where was all her glib repartee? Bess wondered. It was a little difficult to think when she wasn't sure her head was still on her shoulders. "Well," she managed, and settled for that.

"Well." He let her go and added a cocky grin before he walked back to the elevator. Though his stance was relaxed, he was praying the elevator would come quickly, before he lost it and crawled back to her door.

She was still there when the elevator rumbled open. Alex let out a quiet, relieved breath as he stepped inside and leaned against the back wall. "See you around, McNee," he said as the doors slid shut.

"Yeah." She stared at the mural-covered walls. "See you around."

"Holly hasn't been able to stop talking about that party." Judd was scarfing down a blueberry muffin as Alex cruised Broadway. "It made her queen of the teachers' lounge."

"I bet." Alex didn't want to think about Bess's party. He especially didn't want to think about what would be after the party. Work was what he needed to concentrate on, and right now work meant following up on the few slim leads they'd hassled out of Domingo.

"If Domingo's given it to us straight, Angie Horowitz was excited about a new john." Alex tapped his fingers against the steering wheel. "He'd hired her two Wednesdays running, dressed good, tipped big."

Judd nodded as he brushed muffin crumbs from his shirt. "And she was killed on a Wednesday. So was Rita Shaw. It's still pretty thin, Alex."

"So we make it thick." It continued to frustrate him that they'd wasted time interrogating the desk clerks at the two fleabag hotels where the bodies had been found. Like most in their profession, the clerks had seen nothing. Heard nothing. Knew nothing.

As for the ladies who worked the streets, however nervous they were, they weren't ready to trust a badge.

"Tomorrow's Wednesday," Judd said helpfully.

"I know what the hell tomorrow is. Do you do anything but eat?"

Judd unwrapped another muffin. "I got low blood sugar. If we're going to go back and look at the crime scene again, I need energy."

"What you need is—" Alex broke off as he glanced past Judd's profile and into the glaring lights of an all-night diner. He knew only one person with hair that shade of red. He began to swear, slowly, steadily, as he searched for a parking place.

"You really write for TV?" Rosalie asked.

Bess finished emptying a third container of non-dairy product into her coffee. "That's right."

"I didn't think you were a sister." Interested as much in Bess as in the fifty dollars she'd been paid, Rosalie blew out smoke rings. "And you want to know what it's like to turn tricks."

"I want to know whatever you're comfortable telling me." Bess shoved her untouched coffee aside and leaned forward. "I'm not sitting in judgment or asking for confidences, Rosalie. I'd like your story, if you want to tell it. Or we can stick with generalities."

"You figure you can find out what's going on on the streets by putting on spandex and a wig, like you did the other night?"

"I found out a lot," Bess said with a smile. "I found out it's tough to stand in heels on concrete for hours at a time. That a woman has to lose her sense of self in order to do business. That you don't look at the faces. The faces don't matter—the money does. And what you do isn't a matter of intimacy, not even a matter of sex—for you—but a matter of control." She scooted her coffee back and took a sip. "Am I close?"

For a moment, Rosalie said nothing. "You're not as stupid as you look."

"Thanks. I'm always surprising people that way. Especially men."

"Yeah." For the first time, Rosalie smiled. Beneath the hard-edged cosmetics and the lines life had etched in her face, she was a striking woman, not yet thirty. "I'll tell you this, girlfriend, the men who pay me see a body. They don't see a mind. But I got a mind, and I got a plan. I've been on the streets five years. I ain't going to be on them five more."

"What are you going to do? What do you want to do?"

"When I get enough saved up, I'm going South. Going to get me a trailer in Florida, and a straight job. Maybe selling clothes. I look real fine in good clothes." She crushed out her cigarette and lit another. "Lots of us have plans, but don't make it. I will. I'm clean," she said, and lifted her arms, turning them over. It took Bess a minute to realize Rosalie was saying she wasn't a user. "One more year, I'm gone. Less than that, if I hook on to a regular john with money. Angie did."

"Angie?" Bess flipped through her mental file. "Angie Horowitz? Isn't that the woman who was murdered?"

"Yeah." Rosalie moistened her lips before sucking in smoke. "She wasn't careful. I'm always careful."

"How can you be careful?"

"You keep yourself ready," Rosalie told her. "Angie, she liked to drink. She'd talk a john into buying a bottle. That's not being careful. And this guy, the rich one? He—"

"What the hell do you think you're doing?"

Both Rosalie and Bess looked up. Standing beside the scarred table was a tall man with thin shoulders.

There was a cheroot clamped between his teeth, and a diamond winked on his finger. His face was moon-pale, with furious blue eyes. His hair was nearly as white, and slicked back, ending in a short ponytail.

"I'm having me a cup of coffee and a smoke, Bobby," Rosalie told him. But beneath the defiance, Bess recognized the trickle of fear.

"You get back on the street where you belong."

"Excuse me." Bess offered her best smile. "Bobby, is it?"

He cast his icy blue eyes on her. "You looking for work, sweetheart? I'll tell you right now, I don't tolerate any loafing."

"Thank you, but no, I'm not looking. Rosalie was just helping me with a small problem."

"She doesn't solve anyone's problems but mine." He jerked his head toward the street. "Move it."

Bess slid out of the booth but held her ground. "This is a public place, and we're having a conversation."

"You don't talk to anybody I don't tell you to talk to." Bobby gave Rosalie a hard shove toward the door.

Bess didn't think, simply reacted. If she detested anything, it was a bully. "Now just a damn minute." She grabbed his sleeve. He rounded on her. Other patrons put on their blinders when he pushed her into the table. Bess came up, fists clenched, just as Alex slammed through the door.

"One move, Bobby," he said tightly. "Just one move toward her."

Bobby brushed at his sleeve and shrugged. "I just came in for a cup of coffee. Isn't that right, Rosalie?"

"Yeah." Rosalie closed her hand over the business card Bess had slipped her. "We were just having some coffee."

But Alex's eyes were all for Bess. She didn't look pale and frightened. Her eyes were snapping, and her cheeks were flushed with fury. "Tell me you want to press charges."

"I'm sorry." With an effort, Bess relaxed her hands. "We were just having a conversation. Nice talking to you, Rosalie."

"Sure." She swaggered out, blowing smoke in Alex's face for effect.

"Take off."

Bobby moved his shoulders again, smirked. "The coffee's lousy here, anyway." He flicked a glance at Bess. "Next time, sweetheart."

Alex waited ten humming seconds after the door swung shut. Without a word, he stalked over to Bess and grabbed her by the arm and hustled her out the door.

"Look, if this is a knight-in-shining-armor routine, I appreciate it, but I don't need rescuing."

"You need a straitjacket."

With murder in his heart, he dragged her half a block.

"In the car," he snapped, opening the back door of the patrol car.

"A cab would be—"

He swore, put a hand on her head and shoved her into the back seat.

Resigned, Bess settled back. "Hi, Judd," she said as he took his place in the passenger seat in front. "How's Holly?"

"Great, thanks." He slanted a look toward his partner. "Ah, she really had a good time at your place."

"I'm glad. We'll have to do it again." Alex whipped out into traffic with enough force to have her slamming back against the seat. Without missing a beat, Bess crossed her legs. "Am I allowed to ask where we're going, or is this another bust?"

"I should be taking you to Bellevue, where you belong," Alex responded. "But I'm taking you home."

"Well, thanks for the lift."

His eyes flashed to hers in the rearview mirror. Her face was still flushed, and her irises were a sharp enough jade to slice to the bone, but she looked more miffed than upset. *Miffed,* he thought with a snort. Stupid word. It fit her perfectly.

"You're an idiot, McNee. And, like most idiots, you're dangerous."

"Oh, really?" She scooted up in the seat so that she could lean between him and Judd. "Just how do you figure that, smart guy?"

"Not only do you go back down to an area you have no business even knowing about—"

"Give me a break."

"But," he continued, "you sit there drinking coffee with a hooker, then pick a fight with her pimp. The kind of guy who'd as soon give a woman a black eye as wish her good-morning."

Bess poked a finger at his shoulder. "I didn't pick a fight with anyone, and if I had, it would be my business."

"That's why you're an idiot."

"Hey, Alex, ease off."

"Keep out of this," Alex and Bess snarled in unison.

"I'm not even here," Judd mumbled, scooting down in his seat.

"It so happens I was conducting an interview." Bess folded her arms on the seat so that she wouldn't give in to the nasty urge to twist Alex's ear. "In a public place," she added. "And you had no right to come bursting in and ruining everything before I'd finished."

"If I hadn't come bursting in, babe, you'd have had your nose broken again."

She scowled, wrinkling her undeniably crooked nose. "I can defend my nose, and anything else, just fine."

"Yeah, anyone can see you're a regular amazon. Ow!" He slapped at her hand and swore the air blue when she gave in and twisted his ear. "The minute I get you out of this car, I'm going to—"

"Uh, Alex?"

"I told you to keep out of it."

"I'm out," Judd assured him. "But you might want to take a look at the liquor store coming up at nine o'clock."

Still steaming, Alex did, then let out a heavy sigh. "Perfect. This makes it perfect. Call it in."

Bess watched, wide-eyed, as Judd radioed in an armed robbery in progress, gave their location and requested backup. Before she could shut her gaping mouth, Alex was swinging to the curb.

"You," he said, stabbing a finger in her face. "Stay in the car, or I swear I'll wring your neck."

"I'm not going anywhere," Bess assured him after she managed to swallow the large ball of fear lodged in her throat. But before the words were out, he and Judd were out of the car and drawing their weapons.

He'd already forgotten her, she realized as she stared at his profile. Before he and Judd had crossed the street, he'd put on his cop's mind and his cop's face. She'd seen hundreds of actors try to emulate that particular look. Some came close, she realized, but this was the real thing. It wasn't grim or fierce, but flat, almost blank.

Except for the eyes, she thought with a quick shudder. She'd had only one glimpse of his eyes, but it had been enough.

Life and death had been in them, and a potential for violence she would never have guessed at.

In the darkened car, she gripped her hands together and prayed.

He hadn't forgotten her. It infuriated him that he had to fight to tuck her into some back corner of his mind. There were innocent people in that store. A man and a woman. He could smell the fear while he was still three yards away.

But he broke his concentration long enough to glance back and make certain she was staying put.

He gestured Judd to one side of the door while he took the other. He didn't have time to worry that the rookie might freeze. Right now they were just two cops, and he had to believe Judd would go with him through the door.

The 9 mm felt warm in his hand. He'd already identified the weapons of the two perpetrators. One had a sawed-off shotgun, the other a wicked-looking .45. He could hear the woman crying, pleading not to be hurt. Alex ignored it. They would wait for backup as long as they could.

He shifted just enough to look inside.

Behind the counter, a woman of approximately sixty stood with her hands at her throat, weeping. A man of about the same age was emptying the cash register as fast as his trembling hands allowed. One of the gunmen grabbed a bottle off a shelf. He ripped off the top and guzzled. Swearing at the old man, he smashed the bottle on the counter and jabbed the broken glass toward his face.

Alex had seen the look before, and he knew they wouldn't be content with the money. "We're going in," he whispered to Judd. "You go low, go for the one on the right."

Pale, Judd nodded. "Say when."

"Don't fire your weapon unless you have to." Alex sucked in his breath and went through the door. "Police!" In the back of his mind he heard the sirens from the backup as the first gunman swung the shotgun in his direction. "Drop it!" he ordered, knowing it was useless. The woman was already screaming before the first shots were fired.

The shotgun blew out a bank of fluorescent lights as the force of Alex's bullet sent the man slamming backward. Alex was getting the second man in his sights when a bullet from the .45 slammed into a bottle inches above his head, spraying alcohol and glass. Judd fired, and stopped being a rookie.

Slowly, with the same blank look on his face, Alex came out of his crouch and studied his partner. Judd wasn't pale now. He was green. "You okay?"

"Yeah." After replacing his weapon, Judd rubbed the back of his hand over his mouth. There was a greasy knot in his stomach that was threatening to leap into his throat. "It was my first."

"I know. Go outside."

"I'm okay."

Alex gave him a nudge on the shoulder. His hand remained there a moment, surprisingly gentle. "Go outside anyway. Tell the backup to call an ambulance."

Bess was waiting beside the car when Alex came out some twenty minutes later. He looked the same, she thought. Just the same as he'd looked when he walked in. Then he lifted his head and looked at her, and she saw she was wrong.

His eyes hadn't looked so tired, so terribly tired, twenty minutes before.

"I told you to stay in the car."

"I did."

"Then get back in."

Gently she laid a hand on his arm. "Alexi, you made your point. I'll take a cab. You have things to do."

"I've done them." He skirted the car and yanked open the passenger door. She could almost feel his body vibrating, but when he spoke, his voice was firm, sharp. "Get in the damn car, Bess."

She didn't have the heart to argue, so she crossed over and complied. "What about Judd?"

"He's heading to the cop shop to file the report."

"Oh."

He let the silence hang for three blocks. It hadn't been his first, but he hadn't told Judd that the bright, shaky sickness didn't fade. It only turned inward, becoming anger, disgust, frustration. And you never stopped asking yourself why.

"Aren't you going to ask how it felt? What went through my mind? What happens next?"

"No." She said it quietly. "I don't have to ask when I can see. And it's easy enough to find out what happens next."

It wasn't what he wanted. He didn't want her to be understanding, or quietly agreeable, or to turn those damned sympathetic eyes on him. "Passing up a chance for grist for your mill? McNee, you surprise me. Or can't your TV cop blow away a couple of stoned perps?"

He was trying to hurt her. Well, she understood that, Bess thought. It often helped to lash out when you were in pain. "I'm not sure I can fit it into any of our scheduled story lines, but who knows?"

His hands clenched on the wheel. "I don't want to see you down there again, understand? If I do, I swear I'll find a way to lock you up for a while."

"Don't threaten me, Detective. You had a rough night, and I'm willing to make allowances, but don't threaten me." Leaning back, she shut her eyes. "In fact, do us both a favor and don't talk to me at all."

He didn't, but when he pulled up at her building, the smoke from his anger was still hanging in the air. Satisfied, she slammed out of the car. She'd taken two steps when he caught up with her.

"Come here," he demanded, and hauled her against him. She tasted it, all the violence and pain and fury of what he'd done that night. What he'd had to do. There was no way for her to comfort. She wouldn't have dared. There was no way for her to protest. She couldn't have tried. Instead, she let the sizzling passion of the kiss sweep over her.

Just as abruptly, he let her go. He'd be trembling in a minute, and he knew it. God, he needed...something from her. Needed, but didn't want.

"Stay off my turf, McNee." He turned on his heel and left her standing on the sidewalk.

Chapter Four

"When it comes to murder," Bess mused, "I like a nice, quick-acting poison. Something exotic, I think."

Lori pursed her lips. "If we're going to do it, I really think he should be shot. Through the heart."

Shifting in her seat at the cluttered table, Bess scooped up a handful of sugared almonds. "Too ordinary. Reed's a sophisticated, sensuous cad. I think he should go out with more than just a bang." She munched and considered. "In fact, we could make it a slow, insidious poison—milk a few weeks of him wasting away."

"Nagging headaches, dizzy spells, loss of appetite," Lori put in.

"And chills. He really should have chills." Bess steepled her hands and imagined. "He gives this big cocktail party, see. You know how he likes to flaunt his power and money in the faces of all the people he's dumped on over the years.''

Lori sighed. ''That's why I love him.''

''And why millions of viewers love to hate him. If we're going to take him out, let's do it big. They're all there at Reed's mansion.... Jade, who's never forgiven him for using her sister for his own evil ends. Elana, who's agonizing over the fact that Reed will use his secret file, distorting the information to discredit Max.''

''Mmm...'' Getting into the spirit, Lori gestured with her watered-down soft drink. ''Brock, who's furious that with one phone call Reed can upset the delicate balance of the Tryson deal and cost Brock a fortune. And Miriam, of course.''

''Of course. We haven't seen nearly enough of her lately. Reed's self-destructive ex-wife, who blames him for all her problems.''

''Justifiably,'' Lori pointed out.

''Then there's Vicki, the woman scorned. Jeffrey, the cuckolded husband.'' She grinned. ''And the rest of the usual suspects.''

''Okay. What kind of poison?''

''Something rare,'' Bess mused. ''Maybe Oriental. I'll work on it.'' She scribbled a reminder on a notepad. ''So they all have a motive for killing him. Even the housekeeper, because he seduced her naive, innocent daughter, then cast her aside. Sometime during the party, we see a glass of champagne. The room's in shadows. Close-up on a small black vial. A hand pours a few drops into the glass.''

''We'll see if it's a man or woman.''

''The hand's gloved,'' Bess decided, then realized how ridiculous it would be to wear gloves at a cocktail party. "Okay, okay, we don't see it at the party. Before. There's this box, see? This ornately carved wooden box."

"And the gloved hand opens it. Candlelight flickers off the glass vial as the hand removes it from the bed of velvet."

"That's the ticket. We'll cut to that kind of thing three or four times during the week of the party. Let the audience know it's bad business for somebody."

"Meanwhile, Reed's playing everyone like puppets. Handing out his personal brand of misery, building the pressure to the boiling point, until it explodes on the night of the party."

"It'll be great," Bess assured her. "Throughout the evening, Reed's enjoying himself stirring up old fires, poking at sores. Miriam has too much to drink and gets sloppy and shrill. This provides the perfect distraction for our killer to doctor Reed's champagne. Because it's slow-acting, the symptoms don't begin to show right away. We have some fatigue, a little dizziness, some minor pain. Maybe a rash."

"I like a good rash," Lori agreed.

"By the time he kicks off, it'll be difficult for the cops to pinpoint the time and place when the poison was administered. We just might have the perfect crime."

"There is no perfect crime."

Both Bess and Lori glanced toward the doorway. Alex stood there, his hands tucked in his pockets. There was a half smile on his face, a result of his enjoyment at listening to them plotting a murder. "Besides, if your TV cop didn't figure it out, your viewers would be pretty disappointed."

"He'll figure it out." Bess reached for another almond as she watched him, her bare feet propped on the chair beside her. Alex discovered that the baggy slacks she wore effectively hid her legs but didn't stop him from thinking about them. "Did somebody call a cop?" she asked Lori.

"Not me." Well aware that three was most definitely a crowd, Lori rose. "Listen, I've got to make a call, and I think I'll run up and peek in on the taping. Nice to see you, Detective."

"Yeah." He shifted so that Lori could get through the door, but he didn't step inside. Instead, he glanced around, annoyed with himself for feeling so awkward. "Some place," he said at length.

Bess's lips curved. The room was hardly bigger than a closet and windowless. The table where she and Lori worked was covered with books, folders and papers, and dominated by a word processor that was still humming. Besides the table, there was one overstuffed chair, a small couch and two televisions.

"We call it home," Bess said, and tilted her head. "So, what brings you down to the dungeons, Alexi?"

The description was fairly apt. They were in the basement of the building that held the studios and production offices for 'Secret Sins' and its network. He shrugged off her question with one of his own. "How long are you in for?"

"The duration, I hope." Casually she rubbed the ball of one foot over the instep of the other. "After the last Emmy, they did offer us an upstairs office with a view, but Lori and I are creatures of habit. Besides, who's going to come down here and peek over our shoulders while we write?" She recrossed her ankles. "Are you off-duty?"

"I took a couple hours personal time."

"Oh." She drew the word out, thinking he looked very appealing when he was embarrassed. "Should I consider this a personal visit?"

"Yeah." He stepped inside, then regretted it. There wasn't enough room to wander around. "Listen, I just wanted to apologize."

It was probably very small of her, Bess thought, but, oh, she was enjoying this. "Generally or specifically?"

"Specifically." He shook his head when she held out the bowl of almonds. "After the robbery attempt, when I took you home. I was out of line."

"Okay." She set the bowl down and smiled at him. "We're dealing with your behavior during the last half hour of the evening."

His brows drew together. "Everything I said before that sticks. You had no business doing what you were doing, where you were doing it."

"Get back to the apology. I like that better."

"I took what I was feeling out on you, and I'm sorry." Figuring the worst was over, he sat on the edge of the table. "You didn't react the way I expected."

"Which was?"

"Scared, outraged, disgusted." He shrugged again. "I don't usually take women to armed robberies."

Now things were getting interesting. "Where *do* you take them?"

His gaze locked on hers. He knew when he was being teased, and he knew when it was good-natured. "To dinner, to the flicks, dancing. To bed."

"Well, armed robbery is probably more exciting. At least than the first three." She rose, placed her hands on his shoulders and kissed him lightly on the mouth.

"No hard feelings." When his hands came to her hips and held her in place, she lifted a brow. "Was there something else?"

"I've been thinking about you."

"That could be good."

His lips twitched. "I haven't decided that yet. Maybe we could start with dinner."

"Start what?"

"Working our way to bed. That's where I want you."

"Oh." Her breath came out a little too quickly and not quite steady. It didn't help that his eyes were calm, amused and very confident. How, she wondered, had their positions been so neatly reversed? "That's certainly cutting to the chase."

"You said once that people in our professions observe people. What I've observed about you, McNee, is that you'd probably see through any flowers and moonbeams I might toss at you."

Slowly she ran her tongue over her teeth. "Depends on your pitching arm. The idea isn't without its appeal, Alexi, but I prefer taking certain aspects of my life—sex being one of them—in a cautious, gradual manner."

He grinned at her. "That could be good."

She had to laugh. "Meanwhile—" But he didn't let her scoot back.

"Meanwhile," he echoed, keeping his hands firm. "Have dinner with me. Just dinner."

Hadn't she told herself she wasn't going to get involved again, fall in love again? Oh, well. "I often enjoy just dinner."

"Tomorrow. I'm on tonight."

"Tomorrow's fine."

He nudged her an inch closer. "I'm making you nervous."

"No, you're not." Yes, he was.

"You're wriggling." He grinned again, surprised at how satisfying it was to know he'd unsettled her.

"I've got work, that's all."

"Me too. Why don't I come by about seven-thirty? My brother-in-law's got this place. I think you'll get a kick out of it."

"Lady clothes or real clothes?"

"What are you wearing now?"

She glanced down at her sweater and slacks. "Real ones."

"That'll do." He stood, then tilted her chin with a finger until they were eye-to-eye. "You have the oddest face," he said half to himself. "You should be ugly."

She laughed, unoffended. "I was. I've burned all pictures of me before the age of eighteen." Her dimple winked out as she smiled at him. "I imagine you were always gorgeous."

He winced, though he knew he should be used to having that term applied to him. "My sisters were gorgeous," he told her. "Are. My brother and I are ruggedly attractive."

"Ah, manly men."

"You got it."

"And you grew up surrounded by flocks of adoring females."

"We started with flocks and moved on to hordes."

Her eyes lit with amusement and curiosity. "What was it like to—"

He cut her off the most sensible way. He liked the quick little jolt her body gave before she settled into him. And the way her mouth softened, accepted. No pretenses here, he thought as she gave a quiet sigh and melted into the kiss. It was simple and easy, as basic as breathing.

If his system threatened to overcharge, he knew how to control it. Perhaps he drew the kiss out longer than he'd intended to, deepened it more than he had planned. But he was still in control. Maybe, for just a moment, he imagined what it would be like to lock the door, to sweep all those papers off the table and take her, fast and hot, on top of it.

But he wasn't a maniac. He reminded himself of that, even as his blood began to swim. A slow and gentle touch brought pleasure to both, and let a woman see that she was appreciated for everything she was.

"Dangerous," he murmured in Ukrainian as he slid his mouth from her. "Very dangerous woman."

"What?" She blinked at him with eyes that were arousingly unfocused and heavy. "What does that mean?"

He had to make a conscious effort to keep his hands gentle at her shoulders. "I said I have to go. Keep off the streets, McNee."

She called to him as he reached the doorway. "Detective." Her heart was thumping, her head was reeling, but she really hated not having the last word. For lack of anything better, she dredged up an old line from "Hill Street Blues." "Let's be careful out there."

Alone, she lowered herself into a chair, as carefully as an elderly aunt. Five minutes later, Lori found her in exactly the same spot, still staring into space.

"Uh-oh." One look had Lori dropping down beside her. With a shake of her head, she handed Bess a fresh soft drink. "I knew it. I knew this was going to happen the minute I saw that gorgeous cop at your party."

"It hasn't happened yet." Bess took a long drink. Funny, she hadn't realized how dry her throat had become. "I'm afraid it's going to, but it hasn't happened yet."

"You had that same look on your face when you fell for Charlie. And for Sean. And Miguel. Not to mention—"

"Then don't." Frowning, she focused on Lori. "Miguel? Are you certain? I was sure I had better taste."

"Miguel," Lori said ruthlessly. "Granted, you came to your senses within forty-eight hours, but the day after he took you to the opera you had the same stupid look on your face."

"We saw *Carmen*," Bess pointed out. "I don't think the look had anything to do with him. Besides, I'm not in love with Alexi, I'm just having dinner with him tomorrow."

"That's what you always say. Like with George."

Bess's shoulders straightened. "George was the sweetest man I've ever known. Being engaged to him taught me a lot about understanding and compassion."

"I know. You were understanding enough to be godmother to his firstborn."

"Well, after all, I did introduce him to Nancy."

"And he promptly dumped you and ran off with her."

"He didn't dump me. I wish you wouldn't hold that against him, Lori. Breaking our engagement was a mutual decision."

"And the best thing to happen to you. George was a wimp. A whiny wimp."

Because it was precisely true, Bess sighed. "He just needed a lot of emotional support."

"At least you never slept with him."

"He was saving himself."

They looked at each other and burst out laughing. Once she caught her breath, Bess shook her head. "I should never have told you that. It was indiscreet."

"Observation," Lori announced, and Bess gestured a go-ahead. "The cop isn't going to save himself."

"I know." Bess felt the warning flutter in her stomach. Thoughtfully she drew her finger down through the moisture on the bottle. "I'll cross that bridge when I come to it."

"Bess, you don't cross bridges, you burn them." Lori gave her hand a quick squeeze. "Don't get hurt."

There was a touch of regret in Bess's smile. "Do I ever?"

Alex liked the way she looked. It took a certain panache, he supposed, to be able to wear the jade-toned blouse with bright blue slacks, particularly if you were going to add hot-pink high-tops. But Bess pulled it off. Everything about her was vivid. He supposed that was why he'd gone into her office to apologize and ended up asking her out.

It was probably why he hadn't been able to get her, or the idea of taking her to bed, out of his mind since he'd met her.

For herself, Bess took one look at Zackary Muldoon's bar, Lower the Boom, and knew she had a relaxed, enjoyable evening in store. There was music from the juke box, a babble of voices, a medley of good, rich scents. The tangle of pear-shaped gemstones at her ears swung as she turned to Alex. "This is great. Is the food as good as it smells?"

"Better." He gave a wave in the general direction of the bar as he found them a table.

As usual, the bar was cluttered with people and thick with noise. Since his sister had married Zack, Alex had made a habit of dropping in once a week or so, and he knew most of the regulars by name. He grinned at the waitress who stopped at their table. "Hey, Lola. How's it going?"

"It'll do, cutie." Resting her tray on her hip, Lola gave Bess the once-over. Though less than ten years Alex's senior, Lola had taken a maternal interest in him. It wasn't often Alex brought a date into the bar, and Lola made it her business to check out his current lady. "So, what can I get you?"

"Tequila." Bess dropped her bag in the empty chair beside her with a thunk. "Straight up."

Alex only lifted a brow at Bess's choice. "Give me a beer, Lola. Rachel around?"

"Upstairs. And she better have her feet up." She gave the ceiling a scowl. "She'll probably sneak down here before the night's over. Can't keep her away from the boss."

"What's Rio's special tonight?"

"Paella." Her eyes lit with appreciation. She'd sampled some herself. "He's been driving Nick crazy, making him shell shrimp."

"You game for that?" Alex asked Bess.

"You bet." As Lola wandered off, Bess propped her chin on her hands. "So, who's the boss, who's Rio, and who's Nick?"

"Zack's the boss." He gestured toward the tall, broad-shouldered man working the bar. "Rio's the cook, this Jamaican giant who'll fix you the best meal this side of heaven. Nick's Zack's brother."

Bess nodded. She liked to know the players. "And Rachel's married to Zack." After a long study of the man behind the bar, she smiled. "Impressive. How'd she meet him?"

"She was Nick's PD after I busted him for attempted burglary."

Bess didn't blink or look shocked, she simply leaned a little closer. "What was he stealing?"

Alex was vaguely disappointed that he hadn't gotten a reaction. "Electronics—and doing a poor job of it. He was tangled up with a gang at the time. This was about a year and a half ago." Absently he toyed with the square-cut aquamarine on her finger, watching it catch the light. "Nick had some problems. Actually, he's Zack's stepbrother. Nick was still a kid when Zack went off and joined the navy and his mother died. Anyhow, when Zack came back a few years ago, his father was dying, and the kid was chin-deep in trouble."

"This is great." Bess beamed up at Lola as their drinks were served. "Thanks."

The smile did it. Lola sent Alex a look of approval before she swung by the bar to report to Zack.

"Don't stop now."

Alex lifted his mug of beer. He knew very well that Lola was giving Zack a sotto voce rundown of her impressions and opinions of his choice of companion. "You want to hear the whole thing?"

"Of course I do." Bess sprinkled salt on her wrist, licked it, then tossed back the tequila with all the flair of a Mexican bandit. While she sucked on the lime wedge Lola had brought with the drink, she grinned at Zack. "I like the zing."

"How many times can you do that and live?"

"I haven't tested it that far." The liquor left a nice trail of heat down her throat and into her stomach. "I did ten once, but I was younger then, and stupid. So keep going." She leaned forward again. "Zack came back after sailing the seven seas and found his brother in trouble."

"Well, Nick was tangled up with the Cobras..." Alex began. By the time their paella was served, he was enjoying himself. It always polished a man's ego to have a woman's complete and fascinated attention. "So that's how I ended up on the point of having an Irish-Ukrainian niece or nephew."

"Terrific. You've got a flair for storytelling, Alexi. Must be some Gypsy blood in there."

"Naturally."

She smiled at him. All he needed was a hoop of gold in one ear and a violin, she thought—but she was sure he wouldn't want to hear it. "It doesn't hurt that you have this wisp of an accent that peeks out now and then. Of course, your material's first-rate, too. I'm a sucker for happy endings. I can't have many of them in my field. Once we tie things up, we have to unravel them again, or we lose the audience."

"Why? I thought most people went for the happy ending."

"They do. But in soaps, a character loses the edge if he or she isn't dealing with some crisis or tragedy." She sampled the paella and sighed her satisfaction. "That's why Elana's been married twice, had amnesia, was sexually assaulted, had two miscarriages and a nervous breakdown, went temporarily blind, shot a former lover in self-defense, overcame a gambling addiction, had twins who were kidnapped by a psychotic nurse—and recovered them only after a long, heartrending and perilous search through the South American jungles.'' She took another glorious bite. ''Not necessarily in that order.''

Before Alex could ask who Elana was, Lola was setting down fresh drinks. ''You watch 'Secret Sins'?'' she asked Bess.

''Religiously. You?''

''Well, yeah.'' She shrugged, knowing there were several patrons in the bar who'd rag her about it. ''I got hooked when I was in the hospital having my youngest. He's ten now. That was back when Elana was a first-year resident at Millbrook Memorial and in love with Jack Banner. He was a great character.''

''One of the best,'' Bess agreed. ''Brooding and self-destructive.''

''I was really sorry when he died in that warehouse fire. I didn't think Elana would ever get over it.''

''She's a tough lady,'' Bess commented.

''Had to be.'' When someone called her, Lola waved to them to wait. ''If it hadn't been for her, Storm would never have gotten himself together and become the man he is today.''

''You like Storm?''

''Oh, man, who wouldn't?'' With a chuckle, Lola rolled her eyes. ''The guy's every woman's fantasy, you know? I'm really pulling for him and Jade. They deserve some happiness, after everything they've been through. Jeez, all right, Harry, I'm on my way. Enjoy your dinner,'' she said to Bess, and hurried off.

Bess turned to Alex with a smile. "You look confused."

He only shook his head. "You two were talking about those characters as though they were real people."

"But they are," Bess told him, and scooped up some shrimp. "For an hour a day, five days a week. Didn't you ever believe in Batman, or Sam Spade? Scarlett O'Hara, Indiana Jones?"

"It's fiction."

"Good fiction creates its own reality. That's entertainment." Picking up the saltshaker, she grinned. "Come on, Alexi, even a cop needs to fantasize now and then."

He looked at her long enough to make her pulse dance. "I do my share."

Bess swallowed the tequila, but its zing paled beside the one that Alex's quiet statement had streaking through her. "You'll have to tell me about that sometime." She glanced around at the sound of piano music.

Against the far wall was a huge upright. A slimly built, sandy-haired young man was caressing blues out of the keys.

"That's Nick," Alex told her.

"Really?" Bess angled her chair around for a better look. "He's very good."

"Yeah. He talked Zack into putting a piano in the bar about a year ago. Rachel and Muldoon tried to get him to go back to school, get more training, but no dice."

"Some things can't be taught," Bess murmured.

"Looks like. Anyway, he still works in the kitchen with Rio, and comes out and plays when the mood strikes."

"And has every female in the joint mooning over him."

"He's just a kid," Alex said quickly—too quickly.

With her tongue in her cheek, Bess turned back. "Younger men have their own appeal to the experienced woman. In fact, right now Jessica is embroiled in a passionate affair with Tod—who's ten years her junior. The mail is running five to one in favor."

"We were talking about you."

She only smiled. "Were we?"

Zack walked over to slap Alex on the back. "How's the meal?"

"It's terrific." Bess held out a hand. "You're Zack? I'm Bess."

"Nice to see you." Zack kept a hand on Alex's shoulder after giving Bess's a quick squeeze. "You must be the Bess Rachel ran into down at the station."

"I must be. You have a great place here. Now that I've found it, I'll be back."

"That's what we like to hear." His blue eyes sparkled with friendly curiosity. "Alex doesn't bring his ladies around very often. He likes to keep us guessing."

She couldn't help but respond to the humor in Zack's eyes. "Is that so?"

"Ease off, Muldoon," Alex muttered.

"He's still sore at me for stealing his baby sister."

Alex sent him an arched look. "I just figured she had better taste." He lifted his beer. "Speaking of which." He gestured with the mug.

Bess saw Zack's eyes change and, recognizing love, her heart sighed. It didn't surprise her when Rachel came to the table.

"What's this?" Rachel demanded. "A party, and nobody invited me?"

"Sit," Zack and Alex said in unison.

"I'm tired of sitting." Ignoring them both, she turned to Bess. "Nice to see you again." She took a deep, appreciative sniff. "Rio's paella. Incredible, isn't it?"

"Yes, it is. Alex was just telling me how the two of you met."

"Oh?" Rachel's brow lifted.

"Why don't you join us and give me your side of it?"

Twenty minutes later, Alex was forced to admit that Bess's casual friendliness had gotten Rachel to sit down and relax in a way neither he nor Zack would have been able to with their demanding concern.

For a woman who was so full of energy and verve, she had a knack for putting people at ease, he noted.

A gift for listening to details and asking just the right question. And for entertaining, he mused—effortlessly.

It didn't surprise him that she was able to talk music with Nick when he was called over to join them, or food with Rio when she asked to go back into the kitchen to compliment him on the meal. He wasn't surprised when she and Rachel made a date to meet for lunch the following week.

"I like your family," Bess stated as they settled into a cab.

"You've only met a fraction of it."

"Well, I like the one's I've met. How much more do you have?"

"My parents. Another sister, her husband, their three kids. A brother, his wife, and their kid. What about you?"

"Hmm?"

"Family."

"Oh. I was an only child. Do they all live in New York?"

"All but Natasha." He toyed with the curls at the nape of her neck. "You don't talk about yourself."

"Are you kidding?" She laughed, though she wanted to curl like a cat into the fingers brushing her skin. "I never stop talking."

"You ask questions. You talk about things, other people, your characters. But you don't talk about Bess."

She should have known a cop would notice what most people didn't. "We haven't had that many conversations," she pointed out. When she turned her head, her mouth was close to his. She wanted to kiss him, Bess thought. It wasn't merely to distract him. After all, she had nothing to hide. But she didn't speak, only moved her lips to his.

The fingers at the back of her neck tensed as he changed the angle of the kiss and the mood of it. It was light and friendly only for an instant. Then it darkened, deepened, lengthened. Mixed with the taste, the texture, were hints of what was to come.

There's a storm brewing, Bess thought dizzily. And, oh, she'd never been able to resist a storm.

Her heart was knocking by the time his lips moved to her temple. "You know how to change the subject, McNee."

"What subject?"

His hand slid to her throat, cupped there. He felt the pigeon beat of her rapid pulse. The rhythm of it was as seductive as jungle drums. "You. Now I'm only more curious."

"There's not that much to tell." Uneasy and confused by the sensation, she drew back as the cab pulled to the curb. "Looks like we're here." She slid across the seat while Alex paid the driver. Her knees were a little weak, she realized. Another first. Alexi Stanislaski was going to require some thought. "You don't have to walk me up," she said, surprised that it unnerved her to see the cab pull away and leave the two of them alone on the shadowy sidewalk.

"Which means you're not going to ask me in."

"No." She smiled a little, running her fingers up and down the strap of her bag. But she wanted to. It was amazing to her just how much she wanted to. "I think it would be smarter if I didn't."

He accepted that, because the choice had to be hers. And the prospect of changing her mind along the way was tremendously appealing. "We'll do this again."

"Yes."

He closed a hand over her restless one, brought it to his lips. "Soon."

She felt something, a small, vague ache centered in her heart. Confused by it, she slipped her hand away. "All right. Soon. Good night."

"Hold it." Before she could turn away, he took her face in his hands, held it there for a moment before lowering his mouth to hers.

The pressure was whisper-light, persuasive, invasive. Even as she responded, the kiss had that odd ache spreading. Helpless, she brought her hands to his wrists, clinging to them for balance. Though his mouth remained beautifully gentle, the pulse she felt beneath her fingers raced in time with her own.

Then he let her go, stepped back. His eyes stared into hers. "Good night," he said.

She managed a nod before hurrying inside.

There was something about Bess, Alex thought as he waited patiently for the light in her apartment to come on. Something. He'd just have to find out what it was.

Chapter Five

The last person Bess expected to see when she left her office a few days later was Rosalie. Even in the bustling crowds of midtown, the woman stood out. After a moment of blank surprise, Bess smiled and crossed the sidewalk.

"Hi. Were you waiting for me?"

"Yeah."

"You should have come in." Bess adjusted the weight of her bag and briefcase.

"I figured it would be better for you if I waited out here."

"Don't be silly..." Her words trailed off as she tried to see through and around Rosalie's huge tinted glasses. Those sunburst colors around the left eye weren't all cosmetics. Bess's friendly smile faded. "What happened to you?"

Rosalie shrugged. "Bobby. He was a little ticked off about the other night."

"That's despicable."

"I've had worse."

"Bastard." She said it between her teeth, but overlying her fury was a terrible sense of guilt. "I'm sorry. I'm so sorry. It was my fault."

"Ain't nobody's fault, girlfriend. Just the way things are."

"It's not the way they should be. And if I hadn't..." She let that go, knowing you could only go back and change things in scripts. "Do you want to go to the police? I'll go with you. We could—"

"Hell, no." Rosalie let out what passed for a laugh. "I'd get a lot worse than a sore eye if I tried that. And if you think there's a cop alive who gives a damn about a hooker with a black eye, you *are* as dumb as you look."

Alex would care, Bess thought. She refused to believe otherwise. "We'll do whatever you want."

Rosalie pulled out a cigarette, cocking her hip as she lit it. "Listen, you said you'd pay me to talk. I figure I can use the extra money. And I'm on my own time."

"All right." Ideas were beginning to stir. "How much do you average a night?"

As a matter of course, Rosalie started to inflate it, but found the lie stuck in her throat. "After Bobby takes his cut, about seventy-five. Maybe a hundred. Business isn't as good as it used to be."

"We'll talk." Distracted, Bess searched for a cab. "We'll never get a taxi at this hour," she mumbled. "I live uptown about twenty blocks. Do you mind walking?"

This time Rosalie laughed full and long. "Girl, walking the streets comes natural to me."

Once they reached Bess's apartment, Rosalie tipped down her shaded glasses and whistled. Unable to resist, she walked to one of the wide windows. She could see a swatch of the East River through other buildings. The sound of traffic was so muted, it was almost musical. A far cry from the clatter and roar she lived with every day.

"My, oh, my, you do live high."

"How about dinner?" Automatically Bess stepped out of her shoes. "We'll order in." Red meat, Bess thought. At the moment, she could have eaten it raw. "Sit down, I'll get us some wine."

Wine, Rosalie thought as she stretched out on the plump cushions of the pit. She figured that sounded just dandy. "You pay for all this just writing stuff?"

"Mostly." On impulse, Bess chose one of the best bottles in her wine rack. "You're not a vegetarian, are you?"

Rosalie snorted. "Get real."

"Good. I want a steak." After handing Rosalie a glass, she picked up the phone to order dinner.

"I can't pay for that."

"I'm buying," Bess assured her, and curled up on the couch. "I need a consultant, Rosalie." It was a risk, but so was breathing, she decided. "I'll give you five hundred a week."

Rosalie choked on the wine. "Five hundred, just to tell you about turning tricks?"

"No. I want more. I want why. I want you to tell me about the other women. What draws them in. What you're afraid of, what you're not. When I ask you a question, I'll want an answer." Her voice was brisk now, all business. "I'll know if you lie."

Rosalie's eyes were shrewd and steady. "You need all that for a TV show?"

"You'd be surprised." It had gone well beyond the show. The bruise on Rosalie's face grated on her. She had caused it, Bess reflected. She would find a way to fix it. "I'm buying a lot of your time for five hundred a week, Rosalie. You might want to take a little vacation from Bobby."

"What I do after I talk to you is for me to say."

"Absolutely. But if you decided you wanted to take a break from the streets, and if you needed a place to stay while you did, I could help you."

"Why?"

Bess smiled. "Why not? It wouldn't cost me any more."

Intrigued, Rosalie considered. "I'll think about it."

"Fine. We can get started right away." She rose to gather up pads, pencils, her tape recorder. "Remember, this is daytime TV, and we can only do so much. I'll have to filter down a great deal of what you tell me. Why don't I fill you in on the story line?"

Rosalie merely shrugged. "It's your nickel."

"Yes, it is." She settled down again, and was weaving the complex and overlapping relationships of Millbrook—to Rosalie's confusion and fascination—when she heard the buzzer for her private elevator. Still talking, she walked over to release the security lock. "So, anyway, the Josie personality is dynamically opposed to Jade. The stronger she gets, the more confused and frightened Jade becomes. She doesn't remember where she's been when Josie comes out. And the lapses are getting longer."

"Sounds like the lady needs a shrink."

"Actually, she'll go to Elana—she's a psychiatrist—but that's down the road a bit. And under hypnosis— Ah, here's the food." At the elevator's ding, Bess opened the door. The smile froze on her face.

"Alexi."

"Don't you bother to ask who it is before you let someone come up?" He shook his head before he caught her chin in his hand and kissed her.

"Yes—that is, not when I'm expecting someone. What are you doing here?"

"Kissing you?" And, at that moment, she wasn't as responsive as he'd come to expect. Then it occurred to him that she'd said she was expecting someone. A man? A date? A lover? His eyes cooled as he stepped back. "I guess I should have called first."

"No. I mean, yes. That is . . . are you off tonight?"

"I go back on in a couple hours."

"Oh. Well." The buzzer sounded again.

"You could always tell him I'm the plumber."

Baffled, she stepped back inside to release the elevator. "Tell who what?"

"The guy on his way up."

"Why should I tell the delivery boy you're a plumber?"

"Delivery boy?" A sound inside the apartment had him edging closer. He wasn't jealous, damn it, he was just curious. "I guess you've already got company," he began, and pushed the door wider.

"Actually, I do." Giving up, Bess gestured him inside. "We were just about to have some dinner."

He looked over at the couch just as Rosalie stood. Caught between them, Bess felt herself battered by double waves of hostility.

"What the hell is she doing here?"

"You called the cops," Rosalie said accusingly before Bess could answer. "You called the damn cops."

"No. No, I didn't."

Rosalie was already striding across the room. Bess knew that if the woman made it to the door she would have lost her chance. "Rosalie." She grabbed her arm. "I didn't call him."

"And why the hell *didn't* you?" Alex tossed back.

"Because it's none of your business." Still gripping Rosalie, Bess swirled on him. "This is my home, and she's my guest."

"And you're a bigger idiot than I thought."

Sizing up the situation, Rosalie relaxed fractionally. "You two got a thing?"

"Yes," Alex shot back.

"No," Bess snapped, then sighed. "Something in between the two," she mumbled. She snatched her wallet out of her bag as she heard the elevator ding. "Excuse me. That's dinner."

While she herded the delivery boy inside to set up the meal, Alex and Rosalie stood eyeing each other with mutual dislike and suspicion.

"What's the game, Rosalie?"

"No game." She flashed a smile that was as feral as a shark's. "I'm a paid consultant. Your lady hired me."

"The hell with that." He paused a moment, studying her bruised eye. "Bobby do that?"

Rosalie angled her chin. "I walked into a door."

"Sure you did." He did care. Bess might have been surprised at how much he cared. Rosalie certainly would have been stunned. But he also knew there were things that couldn't be fixed. "You'll want to watch your step."

"I don't make the same mistake twice."

He turned away from her, his hands balled into fists in his pockets. "McNee, I want to talk to you."

"Oh, just shut up." She didn't bother to look up as she counted out bills. "Can't you see I'm trying to figure the tip? There you go."

"Thanks, lady." The delivery boy tucked the bills away. "Enjoy your dinner."

"There's enough for three," Bess stated, turning toward Alex. "But you're not going to stay if you're rude."

"Rude?" The single word bounced off her ceiling. He was beside her in two strides. "You think it's rude for me to ask you if you've lost your mind when I walk in and find you've invited a hooker to dinner?"

Her eyes narrowed. "Out."

"Damn it, Bess..."

"I said out." She gave him a hefty shove toward the door. "We went on one date," she reminded him. "*One.* Maybe I entertained the idea of something more, but that gives you no right to come into my house and tell me what to do and who to talk with."

He grabbed her hand before she could push him again. "One has nothing to do with the other."

"You're right. Absolutely right. What I should have said is that I run my life, Detective." She snatched her hand away so that she could poke a finger at his chest. "Me. Alone. Get the picture?"

"Yeah." He wondered how she'd like a nice clip on that pointy little chin of hers. "I've got a picture for you." He hauled her up and kissed her hard. No gentle touch, no finesse. All steam heat. It lasted only seconds, but he succeeded in shocking her speechless. "Things change, McNee." Dark, furious eyes pinned her to the spot. "Get used to it."

With that, he stormed out, slamming the door behind him.

"Well." Bess took one breath, then another. Her throat felt scalded. "Of all the incredible nerve. Who the hell does he think he is, marching in here that way?" Hands on her hips, she spun to face Rosalie. "Did you see that?"

"Hard to miss it." Grinning, Rosalie snatched a french fry from a plate.

"If he thinks he's getting away with that—that *attitude*—he's very much mistaken."

"Man's nuts about you."

"Excuse me?"

"Girl, that was one lovesick puppy."

Bess snatched up her wine and gulped. "Don't be ridiculous. He was just showing off."

"Uh-huh. If I had me a man who looked at me like that, I'd do one of two things."

"Which are?"

"I'd either sit back and enjoy, or I'd run for my life."

Frowning, Bess sat down and picked up her fork. "I don't like to be pushed."

"Seems to me it depends on who's doing the pushing." She sat, as well, and dug right into her steak. "He sure is one fine-looking man—for a cop."

Bess stabbed at her salad. "I don't want to talk about him."

"You're paying the tab," Rosalie said agreeably.

With a grunt of assent, Bess tried to eat. Damn cop, she thought. He'd ruined her appetite.

* * *

There was something to be said for beating the hell out of inanimate objects. Alex had always found the therapy of a pair of boxing gloves and a punching bag immeasurably rewarding. With those so easily accessible, he could never figure out why so many people felt the need for a psychiatrist's couch.

Until recently.

Twenty minutes of sweating and pounding hadn't relieved his basic frustration. He often used the gym—in the middle of a difficult case, when one went wrong, when a good arrest turned sour in court. The same ingredients had worked equally well for him whenever he'd fought with family, or friends, or had female problems.

Not this time.

Whatever hold Bess McNee had on him, Alex couldn't seem to punch himself out of it.

"So much energy, so early."

The familiar voice had Alex blinking away the sweat that had dripped through his headband into his eyes. His brother Mikhail, and Alex's ten-month-old nephew, Griff, were standing hand in hand, grinning identical grins.

"Got your papa out early, did you, tough guy?" Alex swung Griff up for a smacking kiss.

Griff babbled out happily. The only word Alex could decipher in the odd foreign language of a toddler was *Mama.*

"Sydney's tired," Mikhail explained. "She has some wheeling and dealing keeping her up at night. This one's an early riser." He ruffled his son's hair. "So I thought we'd come down and lift weights. Right?"

Griff grinned and cocked his elbows. "Papa."

"Your muscle's bigger," Alex assured him.

"Hey, it's the Griff-man!" Rocky, the former lightweight who ran the gym, gave a whistle and held out his wiry arms. "Come see me, champ."

With a squeal of pleasure, Griff wiggled out of Alex's arms to toddle off on his almost steady legs. "Better watch out, Rock," Mikhail called out. "He's slippery."

"I can handle him." With the confidence of a four-time grandfather, he hefted Griff. "We got things to do," he told Mikhail. "Why don't you talk to your brother there and find out why this is the third time this week he's come in to pound on my equipment?"

"Nosy," Alex muttered. "He's worse than an old woman."

Mikhail tilted a brow when Alex went back to pounding the bag. "Speaking of women..."

"We weren't."

"Why do men come to such places as this unless it's to talk of women?" The music of the Ukraine flavored Mikhail's voice. Alex wondered if his brother knew how much he sounded like their father.

"To hit things," he retorted. "To talk dirty and to sweat."

"That, too. So, it is a woman, yes?"

"It's always a damn woman," Alex said between gritted teeth.

"This one's named Bess."

Alex's punch stopped in midswing. Turning, he used his forearm to swipe his brow. "How do you know about Bess?"

"Rachel tells me." Pleased, Mikhail grinned. "She also tells me that this Bess is not beautiful so much as unique, and that she's smart. This isn't your usual type, Alexi."

"She's nobody's type." Alex turned back to the bag, feinted with his right, then jabbed with his left. "Unique," he said with a snort. "That's her, all right. Her face. It was like God was distracted that day and mixed up the features for five different women. Her eyes are too big, her chin's pointed, her nose is crooked." His gloved fist plowed into the bag. "And she has skin like an angel. I touch it and my mouth waters."

"Mmm... I'll have to get a look at this one."

"I've sworn off," Alex told him between grunts. "I don't need the aggravation. She doesn't have all her circuits working at the same time. Maybe Rachel thinks she's smart because she went to college."

"Radcliffe," Mikhail supplied. "She had lunch with Rachel, and Rachel asked."

"Radcliffe?" Letting out a breath, Alex leaned against the bag. "It figures."

"She also told Rachel that the two of you had a... misunderstanding."

"I understood perfectly. Look, maybe she went to some fancy college, but you couldn't fill up a teaspoon with her common sense. I don't need to get involved with someone that flaky."

Mikhail's bark of laughter echoed through the gym. "This from a man who once dated Miss Lug Wrench."

"It was Miss Carburetor."

"Ah, that's different."

A smile twitched, and Alex punched halfheartedly at the bag. Working up a sweat hadn't relaxed him, but five minutes with Mikhail was doing the job.

"Anyway, we're finished before we got started. And both better off."

"Undoubtedly you're right."

"I know I'm right. We'd always be coming at things from different angles. Hers is cross-eyed. She doesn't see anything the way she should."

"A difficult woman."

"Difficult." Alex held out his hands so that Mikhail could unlace his gloves. "That doesn't begin to describe her. She acts so mild and relaxed, you wouldn't think you could rile her with a cattle prod. Then you point out an obvious mistake, for her own good, and she jumps on you with both feet. Kicks you out of the house."

Mikhail tucked his tongue in his cheek. "You're better off without her."

"You're telling me." Alex tossed his gloves aside and flexed his hands. "Who needs unreasonable women?"

"Men."

"Yeah." With a sigh, Alex sent his brother a miserable look. "I want her so much I can't breathe."

"I know the feeling." He punched his brother's sweaty shoulder. "So go get her."

"Go get her," Alex repeated.

"Put her in her place."

A dangerous light, one Mikhail recognized, flickered in Alex's eyes. "Her place. Right."

"Hey!" Mikhail called out when his brother strode off. "The showers are that way."

"I'll catch one at the station. See you later."

"Later," Mikhail agreed. He wandered off to find his son, wondering how soon he would meet this unique, unreasonable woman without common sense.

She sounded perfect for his baby brother.

Bess was never at her best in the morning, and she suspected anyone who was. Her alarm was buzzing when she heard the pounding on her door. She'd been ignoring the first for nearly ten minutes, but the incessant knocking had her dragging herself out of bed.

Bleary-eyed, pulling a skimpy silk robe over an equally skimpy nightshirt, she stumbled to the door. "What the hell?" she demanded. "Is it a fire or what?"

"Or what," Alex told her when she yanked open the door.

Struggling to focus, she dragged a hand through her hair. The robe drooped off one shoulder. "How'd you get up here?"

"Flashed my badge for the security guard." After closing the door behind him, he looked his fill. There was a great deal to be said for a sleepy woman in rumpled white silk. "Get you up, McNee?"

"What time is it?" She turned away, following the scent from her coffeemaker, which was set to brew at 7:20 each morning. "What day is it?"

"Thursday." He followed her weaving progress through the living area and into a big white-and-navy kitchen. There was a huge arrangement of fresh orchids on the center island. Orchids in the kitchen, he thought. Only Bess. "About 7:30."

"In the morning?" Blindly she groped for a mug. "What are you doing here at 7:30 on a Thursday morning?"

"This." He spun her around. The taste of her mouth, warm and soft from sleep, had him groaning. Before she could think—he didn't want either of them to think—he slipped his tongue between her lips to seduce hers. Her body went stiff, then melted, softening against his like candle wax touched by a flame.

Through the roaring of his blood, he heard the crash as the china mug she'd held slipped from her fingers and smashed on the tiles.

Was she still dreaming? Bess wondered. Her dreams had always been very vivid, but this... It wouldn't be possible to feel so much, need so desperately, in a dream.

And she could taste him. Really taste him. A mingling of man and desire and salty sweat. Delicious. His mouth was so hot, so unyielding, just as his hands were through the thin silk she wore.

She could feel the cool tiles beneath her feet, a shivery contrast to the heat roaring around her. Under her palms, his cheeks were rough, arousingly rough. And she heard her own voice, a muffled, confused sound, as she tried to say his name.

"I have to wake up," she managed when his mouth left hers to cruise over her throat. "I really have to."

"You are awake." He had to touch her—just once. However unfair his advantage, he had to. So he cupped her breasts in his hands, molding their firmness through the silk, brushing his thumbs, featherlight, over straining nipples. "See?"

She'd never been the swooning type, but she was afraid this would be a first. "I have to—" She gasped, for as she'd started to step back, he'd swept her up into his arms. A skitter of panic, completely unfamiliar, raced down her spine. "Alexi, don't."

He covered her mouth again, felt her trembling surrender. And knew he could. And could not. "Your feet are bare,'' he said, and set her on the counter. ''I made you drop your cup.''

Shaken, she stared down at the shards of broken crockery. ''Oh.''

''You have a broom?''

''A broom.'' She was awake now, wide-awake. But her mind was still mush. ''Somewhere. Why?''

He was making her stupid, he realized, and grinned. ''So I can clean it up before you cut yourself. Stay there.'' He walked to a likely-looking closet and located a dustpan and broom. Because he was a man whose mother had trained him well in such matters, he went about the sweeping job quickly and competently. ''So, have you missed me?''

''I haven't given you a thought.'' She blew the hair out of her eyes. ''Hardly.''

''Me either.'' He dumped the shards into the trash, replaced the broom and dustpan. ''How about some coffee?''

''Sure.'' Maybe that would help her regain her normal composure. As he poured, she caught a whiff of him over the homey morning aroma. ''You smell like a locker room.''

''Sorry. I was at the gym.'' When he handed her the coffee, she sat where she was and sipped. Half a cup later, she was able to take her first clear-eyed look at him.

He looked fabulous. Rough and sweaty and ready for action. The thick tangle of hair was falling over a faded gray sweatband. His face was unshaven, his NYPD T-shirt was ripped and darkened in a vee down the chest, his sweatpants were loose and frayed at the cuffs. When she lifted her gaze back to his, he smiled.

''Good morning, McNee.''

"Good morning."

He skimmed a finger over her thigh. She was sensitive there, he noted. He could tell by the way her eyes darkened and the pulse in her throat picked up the beat. "I'm not apologizing this time."

"You should be."

"No. I'm right about this." He put a finger over her lips before she could speak. "Trust me. I'm a cop."

He could have all but seduced her in her own kitchen before her eyes were even open, but she had a point to make. Closing a hand over his wrist, she drew his hand away. "My personal decisions, whether they have to do with my professional or my private life, are just that. Personal. I've been making those decisions, right or wrong, for a long time. I don't intend to stop now."

"I'm not going to see you hurt."

"That's very sweet, Alexi." Softening a bit, she brushed a hand through his hair. "I don't intend to be hurt."

"You don't know what you're dealing with. Oh, you think you do," he continued, recognizing the look in her eyes. "But all you know is the surface. There are things that go on in the streets, every day, every night, that you have no conception of. You never will."

She couldn't argue, not with what she saw in his face. "Maybe not. I don't see what you see, or know what you know. Maybe I don't want to. My friendship with Rosalie—"

"Friendship?"

"Yes." The expression on her face dared him to contradict her. "I feel something for her—about her." With a helpless gesture, Bess set her cup aside. "I can't possibly explain it to you, Alexi. You're not a woman.

I can help her. Don't tell me it's a fairy tale to believe
I can save her from the streets and what she's chosen
to be. I've gotten that advice already.''

"From someone with at least half a brain," he surmised. "I had no idea this had gotten so out of hand.
You said you wanted to talk to her for background
stuff for your story."

"That's true enough." But Bess remembered the
bruise on Rosalie's face too well. "Is it so impossible
that I might be able to make a difference in her life?
Has being a cop made you so hard you aren't willing
to give someone a chance to change?"

He gripped her hands, hard. "This isn't about me."

"No," she said, and smiled. "It's not."

He swore and let go of her to pace to the coffee
maker. "Okay, point taken. It's none of my business.
But I'm going to ask for a promise."

"You can ask."

"Don't go out on the streets with her. Don't go
anywhere near Bobby's territory."

She thought of the man with the silver hair and the
vicious eyes. "That I can promise. Feel better?"

"I'm not through. Don't let her up here unless
you're sure she's alone. Meet her down at your office, or in some public place."

"Really, Alexi . . ."

"Please."

She said nothing for a moment, and then, because
she could see how much it had cost him to use that
word, she relented. "All right." Bess scooted away
from the counter, then opened the bread drawer.
"Want a bagel?"

"Sure."

She popped two into the toaster oven before going to the refrigerator for cream cheese. "There's something I should tell you."

"I'm hoping there's a lot of things."

With a puzzled smile, she turned back. "I'm sorry?"

"I want to know about this personal life of yours, McNee. I want to know all about you, then I want to take you to bed and make love with you until we both forget our own names."

"Ah..." It didn't seem to take more than one of those long, level looks of his to make her forget a great deal more than her name. "Anyway..."

"Anyway?" he repeated helpfully as the toaster oven dinged.

"I was going to tell you about Angie Horowitz."

The lazy smile vanished. His eyes went cool and flat. "What do you know about her?"

"Boy, it really does click off," Bess murmured. "I feel like I just stepped into one of those rooms with the two-way mirror and the rubber hoses."

"Angie Horowitz," he repeated. "What do you know about her?"

"I don't know much of anything, but I thought I should tell you what Rosalie told me." She got out plates, then began to spread the bagels generously. "She said that Angie was really happy to have hooked up with this one guy. He'd hired her a couple of times and slipped her some extra money. Treated her well, promised her some presents. In fact, he gave her this little pendant. A gold heart with a crack down the center."

Alex's face remained impassive. There had been a broken neck chain wrapped in Angie's hand when they found her, just as there had been with the first victim. That little detail had been kept out of the press. There hadn't been a heart, he thought now. But someone had broken the chain for a reason.

"She wore it all the time—according to Rosalie," Bess went on. "Rosalie also told me Mary Rodell had one just like it. She was the other victim, wasn't she?" she asked Alex. "She had it on the last time Rosalie saw her alive."

"Is that it?"

Bess was disappointed that he wasn't more pleased with the information. "There's a little more." Sulking a bit, she bit into her bagel. "Angie called the guy Jack, and she bragged to Rosalie that he was a real gentleman, and was built like..." She trailed off, cleared her throat, but her eyes were bright with humor, rather than embarrassment. "Women have colorful terms for certain things, just like men."

"I get the picture."

"He had a scar."

"What kind?"

"I don't know. A scar, on his hip. Angie told Rosalie he got upset when she asked him about it. That's all she told me, Alexi, but I figured the coincidence of the pendants, you might want to know about this guy."

"It never hurts." He gave her an easy smile, though his instincts were humming. "Probably nothing, but I'll look into it." He tugged on her hair. "Do yourself a favor, and don't tell Rosalie you passed this along to me."

"I'm softhearted, Detective. Not softheaded. She thinks you have a really nice butt—but you're still a cop."

He grimaced. "I don't think I like you discussing my anatomy with a—"

"Friend," she supplied, with a warning lift of her brow. "I also had lunch with your sister. We discussed your nasty temperament."

"I heard." He stole her bagel. "Radcliffe, huh?"

"So?"

"So nothing. Want to go dancing with me?"

She debated with herself for almost a full second. "Okay. Tonight?"

"Can't. Tomorrow?"

It meant canceling dinner at Le Cirque with L. D. Strater. That debate took nearly half a second. "That's fine. Sexy or sedate?"

"Sexy. Definitely."

"Good. Why don't you come by around—" She glanced at the clock, stared, then yelped. "Damn it! Now I'm going to be late. I'll owe Lori twenty dollars if I'm late one more time this month." She began pushing Alex out of the kitchen. "It's all your fault. Now beat it, so I can throw on some clothes and get out of here."

"Since you're already late..." He had some very good moves. Even as she shoved him toward the door, he was turning to catch her close. "I can arrange it so you're a lot later."

"Smooth talker," she said with a laugh. "Take a hike."

"You've already lost twenty. I'm just offering to make it worth your while."

"I don't know how I can resist that incredibly romantic gesture, but somehow I find I have the strength."

"You want romance?" There was a gleam in his eyes as he headed for the door. "Tomorrow night. We'll just see how strong you are."

Chapter Six

After spending most of the morning kicking his heels in court, waiting to testify in an assault case, Alex returned to the station to find his partner hip-deep in paperwork. "The boss wants to see you," Judd said through a mouthful of chocolate bar.

"Right." Alex shrugged out of his jacket and dragged off his court-appearance tie. With his free hand, he picked up his pile of messages.

"I think he meant now," Judd said helpfully.

"I got it." As he passed Judd's desk, Alex peeked over his shoulder at the report in the typewriter. "Two *p*'s in apprehend, Einstein."

Judd backspaced and scowled. "You sure?"

"Trust me." He swung through the squad room and knocked on Captain Trilwalter's glass door.

"Come."

Trilwalter glanced up. If Alex often thought he was swamped in paperwork, it was nothing compared to what surrounded his captain. Trilwalter's desk was heaped with it. The overflowing files, stacks of reports and correspondence gave Trilwalter a bookish, accountantlike look. This was enhanced by the half glasses perched on his long, narrow nose, the slightly balding head and the ruthlessly knotted knit tie.

But Alex knew better. Trilwalter was a cop down to the bone, and he might still be on the street but for the bullet that had damaged his left lung.

"You wanted to see me, Captain?"

"Stanislaski." Trilwalter crooked his finger, then pointed it, gesturing to Alex to come in and shut the door. He leaned back in his chair, folded his hands over his flat belly and scowled.

"What the hell is all this about soap operas?"

"Sir?"

"Soap operas," Trilwalter repeated. "I just had a call from the mayor."

Testing his ground, Alex nodded slowly. "The mayor called you about soap operas?"

"You look confused, Detective." A rare, and not entirely humor-filled, smile curved Trilwalter's mouth. "That makes two of us. The name McNee mean anything to you? Bess McNee?"

Alex closed his eyes a moment. "Oh, boy."

"Rings a bell, does it?"

"Yes, sir." Alex gave himself a brief moment to contemplate murder. "Miss McNee and I have a personal relationship. Sort of."

"I'm not interested in your personal relationship, sort of or otherwise. Unless they come across my desk."

"When I arrested her—"

"Arrested her?" Trilwalter held up one hand while he took off his glasses. Slowly, methodically, he massaged the bridge of his nose. "I don't think I have to know about that. No, I'm sure I don't."

Despite himself, Alex began to see the humor in it. "If I could say so, Captain, Bess tends to bring that kind of reaction out in a man."

"She's a writer?"

"Yes, sir. For 'Secret Sins.'"

Trilwalter lifted tired eyes. "'Secret Sins.' Apparently the mayor is quite a fan. Not only a fan, Detective, but an old chum of your Bess McNee's. *Old chum* was just how he put it."

Finding discretion in silence, Alex said nothing as Trilwalter rose. The captain walked to the watercooler wedged between two file cabinets in the corner of his office. He poured out a paper cupful and drank it down.

"His honor, the mayor, requests that Miss McNee be permitted to observe a day in your life, Detective."

Alex made a comment normally reserved for locker rooms and pool halls. Trilwalter nodded sagely.

"My sentiments exactly. However, one of the less appealing aspects of working this particular desk is playing politics. You lose, Detective."

"Captain, we're closing in on that robbery on Lexington. I've got a new lead on the hooker murders and a message on my desk from a snitch who could know something about that stiff we found down on East Twenty-third. How am I supposed to work with some ditzy woman hanging over my shoulder?"

"This is the ditzy woman you have a personal relationship with?"

Alex opened his mouth, then closed it again. How to explain Bess? "Sort of," he said at length. "Look, Captain, I already agreed to talk to McNee about police work, in general, now and again. I never agreed to specifics. I sure as hell don't want her riding shotgun while I work."

"A day in your life, Stanislaski." With that same grim smile, Trilwalter crushed his cup and tossed it. "Monday next, to be exact."

"Captain—"

"Deal with it," Trilwalter said. "And see that she stays out of trouble."

Dismissed, Alex stalked back to his desk. He was still muttering to himself when Judd wandered over with two cups of coffee.

"Problem?"

"Women," Alex said.

"Tell me about it." Because he'd been waiting all morning for the chance, Judd sat on the edge of Alex's desk. "Speaking of women, did you know that Bess was engaged to L. D. Strater?"

Alex's head snapped up. "What?"

"Used to be," Judd explained. "One of the teachers at Holly's school's a real gossip-gatherer. Reads all the tabloids and stuff. She was telling Holly how Strater and Bess were a thing a few months ago."

"Is that so?" Alex remembered how they'd danced together at her party. Kissed. His mouth flattened into a grim line as he lifted the cup.

"A real whirlwind sort of thing—according to my sources. Before that, she was engaged to Charles Stutman."

"Who the hell is that?"

"You know, the writer. He's got that hot play on Broadway now. *Dust to Dust*. Holly really wants to see it. I thought maybe Bess could wangle some tickets."

The sound Alex made was neither agreement nor denial. It was more of a growl.

"Then there was George Collaway—you know, the son of that big publisher? That was about three years ago, but he married someone else."

"The lady gets around," Alex said softly.

"Yeah, and in top circles. And, hey, Holly was really blown away when she found out that Bess was Roger K. McNee's daughter. You know, the camera guy."

"Camera guy?" Alex repeated, feeling a hole spreading in the pit of his stomach. "As in McNee-Holden?"

"Yeah. First camera I ever bought was a Holden 500. Use their film all the time, too. Hell, so does the department. Well." He straightened. "If you get a chance, maybe you could ask Bess about those tickets. It sure would mean a lot to Holly."

McNee-Holden. Alex ran the names over in his head while the noise of the squad room buzzed around him. For God's sake, he had one of their cameras himself. He'd bought their little red packs of film hundreds of times over the years. The department used their developing paper. He was pretty sure NASA did too.

Wasn't Bess just full of secrets!

So she was rich. Filthy rich. He picked up his messages again, telling himself it wasn't such a big deal. Wouldn't have been, he corrected silently, if she'd told him about it herself.

Engaged, he thought with a frown. Three times engaged. Shrugging, he picked up the phone. None of his business, he reminded himself as he punched in numbers. If she'd been married three times, it would be none of his business. He was taking her dancing, not on a honeymoon.

But it was a long time before he was able to shuffle her into a back corner of his mind and get on with his job.

Sexy, the man had said, Bess remembered, turning in front of her cheval glass. It looked as though she were going to oblige him.

Snug teal silk hugged every curve and ended abruptly at midthigh. Over the strapless, unadorned bodice, she wore a short, body jacket of fuchsia. Long, wand-shaped crystals dangled at her ears. After stepping into her heels, she gave her hair a last fluff.

She felt like dancing.

When her buzzer sounded, she grinned at her reflection. Leave it to a cop to be right on time. Grabbing her purse—a small one that bulged with what she considered the essentials—she hurried to the intercom.

"I'll come down. Hold on."

She found him on the sidewalk, looking perfect in gray slacks and a navy shirt. His hands were tucked in the pockets of his bomber jacket.

"Hi." She kissed him lightly, then tucked an arm through his. "Where are we going?"

It gave him a jolt, the way their eyes and mouths lined up. As they would if they were in bed. "Downtown," he said shortly, and steered her left toward the corner to catch a cab.

He couldn't have pleased her more with his choice of the noisy, crowded club. The moment she stepped inside, Bess's blood started to hum. The music was loud, the dancing in full swing. They squeezed up to the bar to wait for a table.

"Vodka, rocks," Alex ordered, raising his voice over the din.

"Two," Bess decided, and smiled at him. "I think I was here before, a few months ago."

"I wouldn't be surprised." Not his business, Alex reminded himself. Her background, the men in her life. None of it.

The hell it wasn't.

"It doesn't look like the kind of place Strater would bring you."

"L.D.?" Her eyes laughed. "No, not his style." She angled herself around. "I love to watch people dance, don't you? It's one of the few legal forms of exhibitionism in this country." When he handed her her drink, she murmured a thank-you. "Take that guy there." She gestured with the glass at a man who was strutting on the floor, thumbs in his belt loops, hips wiggling. "That's definitely one of the standard urban white male mating dances."

"Did you do a lot of dancing with Stutman?" Alex heard himself ask.

"Charlie?" She sampled the vodka, pursed her lips. "Not really. He was more into sitting in some smoky club listening to esoteric music that he could obsess to." Still scanning the crowd, she caught the eye of a man in black leather. He cocked a brow and started toward her. One hard look from Alex, and he veered away.

Bess chuckled into her glass. "That put him in his place." Rattling her ice, she grinned up at him. "Were you born with that talent, or did you have to develop it?"

Alex plucked the glass out of her hand and set it aside. "Let's dance."

Always willing to dance, Bess let him pull her onto the floor. But instead of bopping to the beat, he wrapped his arms around her. While legs flashed and arms waved around them, and the music rocked, they glided.

"Nice." Smiling into his eyes, she linked her arms around his neck. "I see why you like to make your own moves, Detective."

"I believe I promised you romance." He skimmed his lips over her jaw to her ear.

"Yes." Her breath came out slow and warm as she closed her eyes. "You did."

"I'm not sure what a woman like you considers romantic."

Her skin shivered under his lips. "This is a good start."

"It's tough." He drew away so that their lips were an inch apart. "It's tough for a cop to compete with tycoons and playwrights."

Her eyes were half-closed and dreamy through her lashes. "What are you talking about?"

"A couple of your former fiancés."

The lashes lifted fractionally. "What about them?"

"I wondered when you were going to mention them. Or the fact that your father runs one of the biggest conglomerates known to man. Or the little detail about your chum the mayor calling my captain."

They continued to dance as he spoke, but Bess could see the anger building in his eyes. "Do you want to take them as separate issues, or all in one piece?"

She was a cool one, he thought. He was feeling anything but cool. "Why don't we start with the mayor? You had no right."

"I didn't ask him to call, Alexi." She spoke carefully, feeling the taut strength of his fingers at her waist. "We were having dinner, and—"

"You often have dinner with the mayor?"

"He's an old family friend," she said patiently. "I was telling him how helpful you'd been, and one thing led to another. I didn't know he'd called your captain until after it was done. I admit I liked the idea, and if it's caused you any trouble, I'm sorry."

"Great."

"My work's as important to me as yours is to you," she shot back, struggling with her own temper. "If you'd prefer, I can arrange to spend Monday observing another cop."

"You'll spend Monday where I can keep my eye on you."

"Fine. Excuse me." She broke away and worked her way through the crowd to the rest room. The music pulsed against the walls as she paced the small room, ignoring the chatter from the two women freshening their lipstick at the mirror. Losing her temper would be unproductive, she reminded herself. Better, much better, to handle this situation calmly, coolly.

When she was almost sure she could, she walked back out.

He was waiting for her. Taking her arm, he led her to a table in the rear, where they could talk without shouting.

"I think we should go. There's no use staying when you're so angry with me," she began, but he merely scraped back her chair.

"Sit."

She sat.

"When were you going to tell me about your family?"

"I don't see it as an issue." And that was true enough. "Why should it be? This is only the second time we've gone out."

The look he sent her had her jiggling a foot under the table. "You know damn well there's more going on between us than a couple of dates."

"All right, yes, I do." She picked up her drink, then set it down again, untouched. "But that's not the point. You're acting as though I deliberately hid something from you, or lied. That's just not true."

He picked up the fresh drink he'd ordered. "So tell me now."

"What? Didn't you run a make on me?" His narrowed eyes gave her some small sense of satisfaction. "Okay, Detective, I'll fill you in since you're so interested. My family owns McNee-Holden, which, since its inception in 1873, has expanded from still cameras and film to movies, television, satellites, and all manner of things. Shall I have them send you a prospectus?"

"Don't get smart."

"I'm just warming up." She hooked an arm over the back of her chair. "My father heads the company, and my mother entertains and does good works. I'm an only child, who was born rather late in life to them. My father's name is Roger, and he enjoys a racketing good game of polo. My mother's name is

Susan—never Sue or Susie—and she prefers a challenging rubber of bridge. What else would you like to know?''

Despite his temper, he wanted to take her hand and soothe her. "Damn it, Bess, it isn't an interrogation."

"Isn't it? Let me make it easy for you, Alexi. I was born in New York, spent the early part of my childhood on our estate on Long Island, in the care of a very British nanny I was extremely fond of, before going off to boarding school. Which I detested. This, however, left my mother free to pursue her many charitable causes, and my father free to pursue his business. We are not close. From time to time we did travel together, but I was not a pretty child, nor a tractable one, and my parents usually left my care up to the servants."

"Bess—"

"I'm not finished." Her eyes were hard and bright. "This isn't a poor-little-rich-girl story, Alexi. I wasn't neglected or unhappy. Since I had no more in common with my parents than they had with me, I was content to go my own way. They don't interfere, and we get along very well. Because I prefer making my own way, I don't trumpet the fact that I'm Roger K. McNee's little girl. I don't hide it, either—otherwise, I would have changed my name. It's simply a fact. Satisfied?"

He took her hand before she could rise. His voice was calm again, and too gentle to resist. "I wanted to know who you are. I have feelings for you, so it matters."

Slowly her hand relaxed under his. The hard gleam faded from her eyes. "I understand that someone with your background would feel that their family, who and what they came from, are part of what they are. I don't feel that way about myself.''

''Where you come from means something, Bess.''

''Where you are means more. What does your father do?''

''He's a carpenter.''

''Why aren't you a carpenter?''

''Because it wasn't what I wanted.'' He drummed his fingers on the table as he studied her. ''Your point,'' he acknowledged. ''Look, I'm sorry I pushed. It was just weird hearing all this from Judd.''

''From Judd?''

''He got it from Holly, who got it from some other teacher who reads the tabloids.'' Even as he said it, it struck him as ridiculous. He grinned.

''See?'' Relaxed again, she leaned forward. ''Life really is a soap opera.''

''Yours is. *Three* ex-fiancés?''

''That depends on how you count.'' She took Alex's hand, because she liked the feel of it in hers. ''I wasn't engaged to L.D. He did give me a ring, and I didn't have the heart to tell him it was ostentatious. But marriage wasn't discussed.''

''One of the ten richest men in the country gave you an ostentatious ring, but marriage wasn't discussed?''

''That's right. He's a very nice man—a little pompous, sometimes, but who wouldn't be, with so many people ready to grovel? Can we get some chips or something?''

''Sure.'' He signaled to a waitress. ''So you didn't want to marry him.''

''I never thought about it.'' Since he asked, she did so now. ''No, I don't think I would have liked it very much. He wouldn't have either. L.D. finds me amusing and a little unconventional. Being a tycoon isn't all fun and games, you know.''

''If you say so.''

She chuckled. ''But he'd prefer a different type for his next wife.'' She dived in immediately when the waitress set baskets of chips and pretzels on the table. ''I enjoyed being in love with him for a few weeks, but it wasn't the romance of the century.''

''What about the other one, the writer?''

''Charlie.'' There was a trace of wistfulness now. ''I was really stuck on Charlie. He has this kind of glow about him. He's so interested in people, in emotions, in motivations.'' She gestured with half a pretzel. ''The thing about Charlie is, he's good. Deep-down good. Entirely too good for me.'' She finished off the pretzel. ''See, I do things like join Greenpeace. Charlie flies to Alaska to help clean up oil spills. He's committed. That's why Gabrielle is perfect for him.''

''Gabrielle?''

''His wife. They met at a whale rally. They've been married almost two years now.''

Alex was determined to get it right. ''You were engaged to a married man?''

''No.'' Insulted, she poked out her lip. ''Of course not. He got married after we were engaged—that is, after we weren't engaged anymore. Charlie would never cheat on Gabrielle. He's too decent.''

''Sorry. My mistake.'' He considered changing the subject, but this one was just too fascinating. ''How about George? Was he between Charlie and Strater?''

''No, George was before Charlie and after Troy. Practically in another life.''

"Troy? There was another one?"

"Oh, you didn't know about him." She propped her chin on her hand. "I guess your source didn't dig back far enough. Troy was while I was in college, and we weren't engaged for very long. Only a couple of weeks. Hardly counts."

Alex picked up his drink again. "Hardly."

"Anyway, George was a mistake—though I'd never admit it to Lori. She gloats."

"George was a mistake? The others weren't?"

She shook her head. "Learning experiences. But George, well... I was a little rash with him. I felt sorry for him, because he was always sure he was coming down with some terminal illness, and he'd been in therapy since kindergarten. We should never have gotten involved romantically. I was really relieved when he decided to marry Nancy instead."

"Is this like a hobby?" Alex asked after a moment.

"No, people plan hobbies. I never plan to fall in love. It just happens." Her smile was amused and tolerant. "It feels good, and when it's over, no one's hurt. It isn't a sexual thing, like with Vicki. She goes from man to man because of the sense of sexual power it gives her. I know most people think if you have a relationship with a man—particularly if you're engaged to him—you must be sleeping with him. But it's not always true."

"And if you're not engaged to him?"

Because the question demanded it, she met his eyes levelly. "Every situation has its own rules. I don't know what they are for this one yet."

"Things may get serious."

There was a slight pressure around her heart. "That's always a possibility."

"They're serious enough right now for me to ask if you're seeing anyone else."

She knew it was happening. Bess had never been able to prevent that slow, painless slide into love. "Are you asking me if I am, or are you asking me not to?"

It wasn't painless for him. It was terrifying. With what strength of will he had left, Alex held himself on that thin, shaky edge. "I'm asking you not to. And I'm telling you that I don't want anyone else. I can't even think of anyone else."

Her eyes were warm as she leaned over to touch her lips to his. "There is no one else."

He laid a hand on her cheek to keep her mouth on his for another moment. Even as he kissed her, he wondered how many other men had heard her say those same words.

He told himself he was a jealous idiot. With an effort, he managed to smother the feeling. Rising, he took her hands and pulled her to her feet.

"We're supposed to be dancing."

"So I was told. Alexi." Snuggling into love as she would have into a cozy robe, she cupped his face in her hands.

"What?"

"I'm just looking. I want to make sure you're not mad at me anymore."

"I'm not mad at you." To prove it, he kissed the tip of her crooked nose.

No, not angry, she thought, searching his eyes. But there was something else shadowed there. She couldn't quite identify it. "My middle name's Louisa."

With a half smile on his lips, he tilted his head. "Okay."

"I'm trying to think if there's something else you might want to know that I haven't told you." Needing to be close, she rested her cheek against his. "I really don't have any secrets."

He turned his face into her hair. God, what was she doing to him to tie him up in knots like this? He pulled her against him, wrapping his arms tight around her. "I know all I need to know," he said quietly. "We're going to have to figure out those rules, Bess. We're going to have to figure them out fast."

"Okay." She wasn't sure what was holding her back. It would have been so easy to hurry out of the club with him, to go home and be with him. Her body was straining for him. And yet . . .

The first tremor of panic shocked her enough to have her pull back and smile, too brightly. She wasn't afraid, she assured herself. And she didn't need to overanalyze. When the time was right to move forward, she'd know it. That was all.

"Come on, Detective." Still smiling, she pulled him away from the table. "Let's see if you can keep up with me on the dance floor."

Chapter Seven

Alex read over a particularly grisly autopsy report on half of a suspected murder-suicide, and tried to ignore the fact that Bess was sitting in a chair to his right, scribbling in her notebook. She was as good as her word, he was forced to admit. Though she did tend to mumble to herself now and again, she was quiet, unobtrusive, and once she'd realized he wouldn't answer her questions—much less acknowledge her presence—she'd directed them to Judd.

He couldn't say she was a problem. But, of course, she *was* a problem. She was there. And because she was there, he thought about her.

She'd even dressed quietly, in bone-colored slacks and a navy blazer. As if, he thought, the conservative clothes would help her fade into the background and make him forget she was bothering him. Fat chance, when he was aware of her in every cell.

He could smell her, couldn't he? he thought, seething with resentment. That fresh and seductive scent had been floating at the edges of his senses all morning. Sneaking into his brain the way a good second-story man sneaks through a window.

And he could sense her, too. He didn't need a cop's instincts to know she was behind him, to picture those big green eyes drawing a bead on his every move. To imagine those never-still hands making notes, or that soft, agile mouth curving when a fresh idea came to her.

She could have dressed in cardboard and made him needy.

He was so damn cute, Bess was thinking, smiling at the back of his head. She enjoyed watching him work—the way he scooped his hand through all that gorgeous black hair when he was trying to think. Or shifted the phone from one ear to the other so that he could take notes. The sound of his voice, clipped and no-nonsense or sly and persuasive, depending on what he wanted from the listener.

And she particularly enjoyed the way he moved his shoulders, restlessly, annoyance in every muscle, when he became too aware of her presence.

She had a terrific urge to press a kiss to the back of his neck—and to see what he was reading.

After a couple of scowls from him, she scooted her chair back and stopped peeking over his shoulder.

She was cooperating fully, Alex was forced to admit. Which only made it worse. He wanted her to go away. How could he explain that it was impossible for him to concentrate on his job when the woman he was falling in love with was watching him read an autopsy report?

"Here you go." Bess gave him a cup of coffee and a friendly smile. "You look like you could use it."

"Thanks." Cream, no sugar, he noted as he sipped. She'd remembered. Was that part of her appeal? he wondered. The fact that she absorbed those little details about people? "You must be getting bored."

Taking a chance, she sat on the edge of his desk. "Why?"

"Nothing much going on." He gestured to indicate the pile of paperwork. Maybe, just maybe, he could convince her she was wasting her time. "If you have your TV cop doing this, it isn't going to up your ratings."

"We'll want to show different aspects of his work." She broke a candy bar in half and offered Alex a share. "Like the fact that he'd have to concentrate and handle this sort of paperwork and detail in the middle of all this chaos."

He took a bite. "What chaos?"

She smiled again, jotting down notes. He didn't even see it any longer, she realized. Or hear it. All the noise, the movement, the rush. Dozens of little dramas had taken place that morning, fascinating her, unnoted by him.

"They brought a drug dealer in over there." She gestured with a nod as she continued to write. "Skinny guy in a white fedora and striped jacket, wearing a heavy dose of designer cologne."

"Pasquale," Alex said, noting the description. "So?"

"You saw him?"

"I smelled him." He shrugged. "Wasn't my collar."

Chuckling to herself, Bess crossed her legs and got comfortable. "A Korean shopkeeper came rushing in shouting about vandalism at his store. He was so excited he lost most of his English. They sent out for an interpreter."

"Yeah, it happens." What was her point? he wondered.

She only smiled and finished her chocolate. "Right after that, they brought in a woman who'd been knocked around by her boyfriend. She was sitting over there—defending him, even while her face was swelling. The detective at the far end had a fight with his wife over the phone. He forgot their anniversary."

"Must have been Rogers. He's always fighting with his wife." Impatience rippled back. "What's that got to do with anything?"

"Atmosphere," she told him. "You've stopped noticing it and become a part of it. It's interesting to see. And you're very organized," she added, licking chocolate from her thumb. "Not like Judd over there, with all his neat little piles, but in the way you spread things out and know just where to find the right piece of paper at the right time."

"I hate having you stare at me when I work." He slapped her hand away from the autopsy report.

"I know." Unoffended, she grinned. She leaned a little closer. There was something in her eyes besides humor, he noted. He wasn't sure if he'd ever seen desire and amusement merged in the same expression before. And he certainly hadn't realized how the combination could make a man's blood hum. "You look very sexy plowing your way through all this, gun strapped to your side, your hair all messed up from

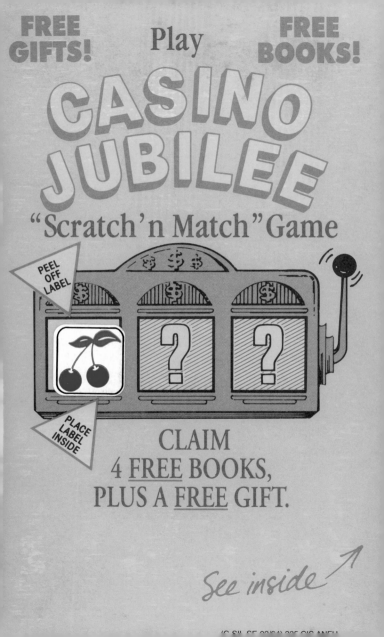

NO RISK, NO OBLIGATION TO BUY...NOW OR EVER!

CASINO JUBILEE
"Scratch'n Match" Game

Here's how to play:

1. Peel off label from front cover. Place it in space provided at right. With a coin, carefully scratch off the silver box. Then check the claim chart to see what we have for you — FREE BOOKS and a gift — ALL YOURS! ALL FREE!

2. Send back this card and you'll receive brand-new Silhouette Special Edition® novels. These books have a cover price of $3.50 each, but they are yours to keep absolutely free.

3. There's no catch. You're under no obligation to buy anything. We charge nothing – ZERO – for your first shipment. And you don't have to make any minimum number of purchases – not even one!

4. The fact is thousands of readers enjoy receiving books by mail from the Silhouette Reader Service™ months before they're available in stores. They like the convenience of home delivery and they love our discount prices!

5. We hope that after receiving your free books you'll want to remain a subscriber. But the choice is yours – to continue or cancel, anytime at all! So why not take us up on our invitation, with no risk of any kind. You'll be glad you did!

YOURS FREE!

This lovely Victorian pewter-finish miniature is perfect for displaying a treasured photograph – and it's yours absolutely free – when you accept our no-risk offer.

CASINO JUBILEE
"Scratch'n Match" Game

CHECK CLAIM CHART BELOW
FOR YOUR FREE GIFTS!

YES! I have placed my label from the front cover in the space provided above and scratched off the silver box. Please send me all the gifts for which I qualify. I understand that I am under no obligation to purchase any books, as explained on the back and on the opposite page.

335 CIS ANFH (C-SIL-SE-03/94)

Name _____

Address _____ Apt._____

City _____ Province_____ Postal Code _____

CASINO JUBILEE CLAIM CHART

🍒 🍒 🍒		WORTH 4 FREE BOOKS AND A FREE VICTORIAN PICTURE FRAME	
🍒 🔔 🍒		WORTH 4 FREE BOOKS	
🔔 🔔 🍒		WORTH 3 FREE BOOKS	CLAIM Nº 1528

0195619199-L2A5X3-BR01

SILHOUETTE READER SERVICE
PO BOX 609
FORT ERIE, ONT.
L2A 9Z9

If offer card is missing, write to: Silhouette Reader Service, P.O. Box 609, Fort Erie, Ontario L2A 5X3

MAIL ▶ POSTE
Canada Post Corporation / Société canadienne des postes

Postage paid   Port payé
if mailed in Canada   si posté au Canada

Business   Réponse
Reply   d'affaires

0195619199   01

raking your fingers through it. That keen, dangerous look in your eyes.''

Mortified, he shifted in his chair. "Cut it out, McNee."

"I like the way your eyes get all dark and intense when you're taking down some important tidbit of information over the phone."

"For all you know, that was my dry cleaner."

"Uh-uh." She took his coffee to wash down the last bite of candy bar. "Tell me something, Alexi. Are you annoyed that I'm here, or are you nervous that I'm here?"

"Both." He rose. There must be something he had to do someplace else.

"That's what I thought." She hooked a finger around the strap of his holster. She wasn't afraid of the gun he wore. In fact, she was counting on talking him into letting her hold it one day. So that she could see how it felt. How he felt when he was forced to draw it. "You know, you haven't even kissed me."

"I'm not going to kiss you. Here."

She lifted her eyes, slowly. There was a definite dare in them. "Why not?"

"Because the next time I kiss you—" watching her, he slid a hand around her throat, his thumb caressing her collarbone, until her cocky smile faded away "—really kiss you, it's just going to be you and me. Alone. And I'm going to keep right on kissing you, and all sorts of other things, until there aren't any more rules. Any more reasons."

Was that what she wanted? She thought it was. Right now, when her skin was humming where his fingers lay, she thought it was exactly what she wanted. But there was something else, some complex mixture of yearning and fear, so unfamiliar it caused her to step back.

"What's wrong, McNee?" Delighted by her reaction, he let his hand slide down her shoulder and away. "Who's making who nervous now?"

"We're supposed to be working," she reminded him. "Not making each other nervous."

"Today, when I go off the clock, so do you."

"Stanislaski."

Alex's eyes stayed on hers another moment before flicking behind her. "Captain."

"Sorry to interrupt your social hour," he said sourly. "I need that report."

"Right here." Even as Alex was turning to reach for it, Bess was offering her hand to Trilwalter.

"Captain, it's so nice to meet you. I'm Bess McNee. I wanted to let you know how much I appreciate the department's cooperation today."

Trilwalter scowled at her a moment, then, remembering, stifled a sigh. "Right. You're the writer." A sneer twisted his mouth. "Soap operas."

"Yes, I am." Her smile made the fluorescents overhead dim. "I wonder... if I can have just a moment of your time? I know you're very busy, so I won't keep you."

He didn't want any part of her. He knew it, she knew it, and so did any of the cops hovering close enough to hear. But riding a desk had taught him that diplomacy was often his only weapon. Besides, once he made his feelings known, she'd be out of his hair and off finding another precinct to haunt.

"Why don't you come into my office, Ms. McNee?"

"Thank you." She shot a grin over her shoulder at Alex as she followed Trilwalter.

"You going to let her go in there alone?" Judd murmured.

"Yeah." Alex bit back a chuckle as he heard the glass of Trilwalter's door rattle. "Oh, yeah. And I'm going to enjoy it."

Ten minutes later, Alex was surprised by a burst of laughter. Swiveling in his chair, he spotted Trilwalter leading Bess out of his office. The two of them were chuckling together like two old friends over a private joke.

"I'm going to remember that one, Bess."

"Just don't tell the mayor where you heard it."

"I know how to respect a source." Still smiling, he glanced over at a slack-jawed Alex. "Detective, you take care of Ms. McNee. Make sure she gets what she needs."

"Sir." He cut his eyes over to Bess. She merely batted her lashes, managing to look about as innocent as a smoking gun. "I have every intention of making certain Ms. McNee gets exactly what she needs."

Bess laid her hand in Trilwalter's. "Thank you again, Donald."

"My pleasure. Don't be a stranger."

"Donald?" Alex said, the moment the captain was out of earshot.

"Yes." Bess made a production out of brushing dust from her sleeve. "That is his name."

"We use several other names for him around here. What the hell did you do in there?"

"Why, we chatted. What else?"

Glancing over her shoulder, Alex noticed money changing hands. The odds had been even that Trilwalter would chew her up, then spit her out, within ten minutes. Since he'd lost twenty on the deal himself, Alex wasn't particularly pleased.

"Sit down and be quiet," he told her. "I've got work."

"Of course."

Before she could take her seat, his phone rang. "Stanislaski. Yeah." He listened a moment, then pulled out his notepad to scribble. "I hear you. You know how it works, Boomer. It depends on what it's worth." Nodding to himself, he replaced the pad. "Yeah, we'll talk. I'll be there. In ten."

When Alex hung up the phone and grabbed for his jacket, Bess was right behind him. "What is it?"

"I've got someplace to go. Judd, let's hit it."

"I'm going with you."

Alex didn't even glance back as he started out. He was already working on tucking her in some far corner of his mind. "Forget it."

"I'm going with you," she repeated, and snagged his arm. "That's the deal."

It surprised him when he tried to shake her off and she wouldn't shake. The lady had a good grip, he noted. "I didn't make any deal."

She could be just as tough and cold-blooded as he, she thought. She planted her feet, angled her chin. "Your captain did. I ride with you, Detective, wherever you may be going. A day in the life, remember?"

"Fine." Frustration vibrated through him as he stared her down. "You ride—and you stay in the car. No way you're scaring off my snitch."

"Want me to drive?" Judd offered as they headed down the steps to the garage.

"No." Alex's answer was flat and left no room for argument. Judd sent Bess a good-natured shrug. Then, because Alex made no move to do so, he opened the back door of their nondescript unmarked car for her.

"Where are we going?" Bess asked, determined to be pleasant.

"To talk to the scum of the earth," Alex shot back as he pulled out of the garage.

"Sounds fascinating," Bess said, and meant it.

She didn't think she'd ever been in this part of town before. Many of the shop windows were boarded up. Those still in business were grubbier than usual. People still walked as though they were in a hurry, but it didn't look as if they had anyplace to go.

Funny, she thought, how Alex seemed to blend with the surroundings. It wasn't simply the jeans and battered jacket he wore, or the hair he'd deliberately mussed. It was a look in the eyes, a set of the body, a twist of the mouth. No one would look twice at him, she thought. Or if they bothered, they wouldn't see a cop, they'd see another street tough obviously on the edge of his luck.

Taking her cue from him, she pulled out her bag of cosmetics, darkening her mouth, adding just a little too much eyeliner and shadow. She tried a couple of bored looks in the mirror of her compact and decided to tease up her hair.

Alex glanced back at her and scowled. "What the hell are you doing to your face?"

"Getting into character," she said blithely. "Just like you. Are we going to bust somebody?"

He only turned away and muttered.

Just his luck, he thought. He wanted to slip into Boomer's joint unobtrusively, and he was stuck with a redhead who thought they were playing cops and robbers.

Unoffended, Bess put away her mirror and scanned the area. Parking wasn't a problem here. Bess decided that if anyone left his car unattended in this neighborhood for above ten minutes, he'd come back and be lucky to find a hubcap.

Alex swung over the curb and swore. He couldn't leave her in the car here, damn it. Any of the hustlers or junkies on the streets would take one look, then eat her alive.

"You listen to me." He turned, leaning over the seat to make his point. "Stay close to me, and keep your mouth shut. No questions, no comments."

"All right, but where—"

"No questions." He slammed out of his door, then waited for her. With his hand firm on her arm, he hauled her to the sidewalk. "If you step out of line, I swear, I'll slap the cuffs on you."

"Romantic, isn't he?" she said to Judd. "Just sends shivers down my spine."

"Keep a lid on it, McNee," Alex told her, refusing to be amused. He pulled her through a grimy door into an airless shop.

It took her a minute to get her bearings in the dim light. There were shelves and shelves crowded with dusty merchandise. Radios, picture frames, kitchenware. A tuba. A huge glass display counter with a diagonal crack across it dominated one wall. Security glass ran to the ceiling. Cutting through it was a window, like a bank teller's, studded with bars.

"A pawnshop," Bess said, with such obvious delight that Alex snarled at her.

"One word about atmosphere, I'll clobber you."

But she was already dragging out her notebook. "Go ahead, do what you have to do. You won't even know I'm here."

Sure, he thought. How would anyone know she was there, simply because that sunshine scent of her cut right through the grime and must? He stepped up to the counter just as a scrawny man in a loose white shirt came through the rear door.

"Stanislaski."

"Boomer. What have you got for me?"

Grinning, Boomer passed a hand over his heavily greased black hair. "Come on, I got some good stuff, and you know I make a point of cooperating with the law. But a man's got to make a living."

"You make one ripping off every poor slob who walks through the door."

"Aw, now you hurt my feelings." Boomer's pale blue eyes glittered. "Rookie?" he asked, nodding at Judd.

"He used to be."

After an appraising look, Boomer glanced over at Bess. She was busy poking through his merchandise. "Looks like I got me a customer. Hang on."

"She's with me." Alex shot him a knife-edged look that forestalled any questions. "Just forget she's here."

Boomer had already appraised the trio of rings on Bess's right hand, and the blue topaz drops at her ears. He sighed his disappointment. "You're the boss, Stanislaski. But listen, I like to be discreet."

Alex leaned on the counter, like a man ready to shoot the bull for hours. His voice was soft, and deadly. "Jerk my chain, Boomer, and I'm going to have to come down here and take a hard look at what you keep in that back room."

"Stock. Just stock." But he grinned. He didn't have any illusions about Alex. Boomer knew when he was detested, but he also knew they had an agreement of sorts. And, thus far, it had been advantageous to both of them. "I got something on those hookers that got sliced up."

Though his expression didn't change, though he didn't move a muscle, Alex went on alert. "What kind of something?"

Boomer merely smiled and rubbed his thumb and forefinger together. When Alex drew out a twenty, it disappeared quickly through the bars. "Twenty more, if you like what I have to say."

"If it's worth it, you'll get it."

"You know I trust you." Smelling of hair grease and sweat, Boomer leaned closer. "Word on the street is you're looking for some high roller. Guy's name's Jack."

"So far I'm not impressed."

"Just building up to it, pal. The first one that was wasted? She was one of Big Ed's wives. I recognized her from the newspaper picture. Now, she was fine-looking. Not that I ever used her services."

"Turn the page, Boomer."

"Okay, okay." He shot a grin at Judd. "He don't like conversation. I heard both those unfortunate ladies were in possession of a certain piece of jewelry."

"You've got good ears."

"Man in my position hears things. It so happens I had a young lady come in just yesterday. She had a certain piece of jewelry she wanted to exchange." Opening a drawer, Boomer pulled out a thin gold chain. Dangling from it was a heart, cracked down the center. When Alex held out a hand, Boomer shook his head. "I gave her twenty for it."

Saying nothing, Alex pulled another bill out of his wallet.

"Seems to me I'm entitled to a certain amount of profit."

Eyes steady, Alex pulled the twenty back an inch. "You're entitled to go in and answer a bunch of nasty questions down at the cop shop."

With a shrug, Boomer exchanged the bill for the heart. He'd only given ten for it, in any case. "She wasn't much more than a kid," Boomer added. "Eighteen, maybe twenty at a stretch. Still pretty. Bottle blonde, blue eyes. Little mole right here." He tapped beside his left eyebrow.

"Got an address?"

"Well, now..."

"Twenty for the address, Boomer." Alex's tone told the man to take it. "That's it."

Satisfied, Boomer named a hotel a few blocks away. "Signed her name Crystal," he added, wanting to keep the partnership intact. "Crystal LaRue. Figure she made it up."

"Let's check it out," he said to Judd, then tapped Bess on the shoulder. She was apparently absorbed in an ugly brass lamp in the shape of a rearing horse. "Let's go."

"In a minute." She turned a smile on Boomer. "How much?"

"Oh, for you—"

"Forget it." Alex was dragging her to the door.

"I want to buy—"

"It's ugly."

Annoyed at the loss, but pleased to have recorded the entire conversation, she sighed. "That's the point." But she climbed meekly into the car and began to scribble her impressions in her book.

Cramped shop. Very dirty. Mostly junk. Excellent place for props. Proprietor a complete sleaze. Alexi in complete control of exchange—a kind of game-playing. Quietly disgusted but willing to use the tools at hand.

By the time she'd finished scribbling, Alex was pulling to the curb again.

"Same rules," he said to Bess as they climbed out of the car.

"Absolutely." Lips pursed, she studied the crumbling hotel. She recognized it as a rent-by-the-hour special. "Is this where she lives?"

"Who?"

"The girl you were talking about." She lifted a brow. "I have ears, too, Alexi."

He should have known. "As long as you keep your mouth shut."

"There's no need to be rude," she told him as they started in. "Tell you what, just to show there's no hard feelings, I'll buy you both lunch."

"Great." Judd gallantly opened the door for her.

"You're so easy," Alex muttered to his partner as they entered the filthy lobby.

"Hey, we gotta eat sometime."

He hated to bring her in here, Alex realized. Into this dirty place that smelled of garbage and moldy dreams. How could she be so unaffected by it? he wondered, then struggled to put thoughts of her aside as he approached the desk clerk.

"You got a Crystal LaRue?"

The clerk peered over his newspaper. There was an unfiltered cigarette dangling from the corner of his mouth and total disinterest in his eyes. "Don't ask for names."

Alex merely pulled out his badge, flashed it. "Blonde, about eighteen. Good-looking. A beauty mark beside her eyebrow. Working girl."

"Don't ask what they do for a living, neither." With a shrug, the clerk went back to his paper. "Two-twelve."

"She in?"

"Haven't seen her go out."

With Bess trailing behind, they started up the steps. To entertain herself, she read the various tenants' suggestions and statements that were scrawled on the walls.

There was a screaming match in progress behind one of the doors on the first floor. Someone was banging on the wall from a neighboring room and demanding—in colorful terms—that the two opponents quiet down.

A bag of garbage had spilled on the stairs between the second and first floors. It had gone very ripe.

Alex rapped on the door of 212, waited. He rapped again and called out. "Crystal. Need to talk to you."

With a glance at Judd, Alex tried the door. The knob turned easily. "In a place like this, you'd think she'd lock it," Judd commented.

"And wire it with explosives," Alex added. He slipped out his gun, and Judd did the same. "Stay in the hall," he ordered Bess without looking at her. They went through the door, guns at the ready.

She did exactly what she was told. But that didn't stop her from seeing. Crystal hadn't gone out, and she wouldn't be walking the streets again. As the door hung open, Bess stared at what was sprawled across the sagging mattress inside. The stench of blood—and worse—streamed through the open doorway.

Death. Violent death. She had written about it, discussed it, watched gleefully as it was acted out for the cameras.

But she'd never seen it face-to-face. Had never known how completely a human being could be turned into a thing.

From far away, she heard Alex swear, over and over, but she could only stare, frozen, until his body blocked her view. He had his hands on her shoulders, squeezing. God, she was cold, Bess thought. She'd never been so cold.

"I want you to go downstairs."

She managed to lift her gaze from his chin to his eyes. The iced fury in them had her shivering. "What?"

He nearly swore again. She was white as a sheet, and her pupils had contracted until they were hardly bigger than the point of a pin. "Go downstairs, Bess." He tried to rub the chill out of her arms, knowing he couldn't. "Are you listening to me?" he said, his voice quiet, gentle.

"Yes." She moistened her lips, pressed them together. "I'm sorry, yes."

"Go down, stay in the lobby. Don't say anything, don't do anything, until Judd or I come down. Okay?" He gave her a little shake, and wondered what he would do if she folded on him. "Okay?"

She took one shaky breath, then nodded. "She's . . . so young." With an effort, she swallowed the sickness that kept threatening to rise in her throat. "I'm all right. Don't worry about me. I'm all right," she repeated, then turned away to go downstairs.

"She shouldn't have seen this," Judd said. His own stomach was quivering.

"Nobody should see this." Banking down on every emotion, Alex closed the door at his back.

She stuck it out, refusing to budge when Judd came down to drive her home. After finding an old chair, she settled into a corner while the business of death went on around her. From her vantage point, she watched them come and go—forensics, the police photographer, the morgue.

Detached, she studied the people who crowded in, asking questions, making comments, being shuffled out again by blank-faced cops.

There was grief in her for a girl she hadn't known, a fury at the waste of a life. But she remained. Not because of the job. Because of Alex.

He was angry with her. She understood it, and didn't question it. When they were finished at the scene, she rode in silence in the back of the car. Back at the station, she took the same chair she'd had that morning.

Hours went by, endlessly long. At one point she slipped out and bought Alex and Judd sandwiches from a deli. After a time, he went into another room.

She followed, still silent, noted a board with pictures tacked to it. Horrible pictures.

She looked away from them, took a chair and listened while Alex and other detectives discussed the latest murder and the ongoing investigation.

Later, she rode with him back to the pawnshop. Waited patiently while he questioned Boomer again. Waited longer while he and Judd returned to the motel to reinterview the clerk, the tenants.

Like them, she learned little about Crystal LaRue. Her name had been Kathy Segal, and she'd once lived in Wisconsin. It had been hard, terribly hard, for Bess to listen when Alex tracked down and notified her parents. Hard, too, to understand from Alex's end of the conversation that they didn't care. For them, their daughter had already been dead.

She'd been nobody's girl. She'd worked the streets on her own. Two months after she moved into the tiny little room with the sagging mattress, she had died there. No one had known her. No one had wanted to know her.

No one had cared.

Alex couldn't talk to Bess. It was impossible for him. Intolerable. He shared this part of his life with no one who mattered to him. It was true that his sister Rachel saw some of it as a public defender but as far as Alex was concerned that was too much. Perhaps that was why he kept all the pieces he could away from the rest of his family and loved ones.

He hated remembering the look on Bess's face as she'd stood in that doorway. There should have been a way to protect her from that, to shield her from her own stubbornness.

But he hadn't protected her, he hadn't shielded her, though that was precisely what he had sworn to do for people he'd never met from the first day he'd worn a badge. Yet for her, for the woman he was—God, yes, the woman he was in love with—he'd opened the door himself and let her in.

So he didn't talk to her, not even when it was time to turn it off and go home. And in the silence, his anger built and swelled and clawed at his guts. He found the words when he stepped into her apartment and closed the door.

"Did you get enough?"

Bess was in no mood to fight. Her emotions, always close to the surface, had been wrung dry by what she'd seen and heard that day. She would let him yell, if that was what he needed, but she was tired, she was aching, and her heart went out to him.

"Let me get you a drink," she said quietly, but he snagged her arm and whirled her back.

"Is it all in your notes?" That cold, terribly controlled fury swiped out at her. "Can you find a way to use it to entertain those millions of daytime viewers?"

"I'm sorry." It was all she could think of. "Alexi, I'm so sorry." She took a deep breath. "I want a brandy. I'll get us both one."

"Fine. A nice, civilized brandy is just what we need."

She walked away to choose a bottle from an old lacquered cabinet. "I don't know what you want me to say." Very carefully, very deliberately, she poured two snifters. "I'll apologize for choosing today to do this, if that helps. I'll apologize for making it more difficult for you by being there when this happened."

She brought the snifter to him, but he didn't take it. "Right now, I'd be willing to say anything you'd like to hear."

He couldn't get beyond it, no matter what she said. He couldn't get beyond knowing he'd opened the door on the kind of horror she'd never be able to forget. "You had no business being there. You had no business seeing any of that."

With a sigh, she set both snifters aside. Maybe brandy wouldn't help after all. "You were there. You saw it."

His eyes flashed white heat. "It's my damn job."

"I know." She lifted a hand to his cheek, soothing. "I know."

Compelled, he grabbed her wrist, held tight a moment before he turned away. "I don't want you touched by it. I don't want you touched by it ever again."

"I can't promise that." Because it was her way, she wrapped her arms around his waist, rested her cheek against his back. He was rigid as steel, unyielding as granite. "Not if you want something between us."

"It's because I do want something between us."

"Alexi." So many emotions, she thought. Always before it had been easy to sort them out, to drift with them. But this time... It had been a long, hard day, she reminded herself. There would be time to think later. "If what you want is someone you can tuck in a comfortable corner, it isn't me. What you do is part of what you are." When he turned, she brushed her hands over his cheeks again, refusing to let him retreat. "You want me to say I was appalled by what I saw in that room? I was. I was appalled by the cruelty of it, sickened by the terrible, terrible waste."

That sliced at him, a long, thin blade through the heart. "I shouldn't have let you go with me. That part of my life isn't ever going to be part of yours."

"Stop." The sorrow that had paled her face hardened into determination. "Do you think that because I write fantasy I don't know anything about the real world? You're wrong. I know, it just doesn't overwhelm my life. And I know that what you faced today you may face tomorrow. Or worse. I know that every time you walk out the door you may not come back." The quick lick of fear reminded her to slow down and speak carefully. "What you are makes that a very real possibility. But I won't let that overwhelm me, either. Because there's nothing about you I'd change."

For a moment, he simply stared at her, a hundred different feelings fighting for control inside him. Then, slowly, he lowered his brow to hers and shut her eyes. "I don't know what to say to you."

"You don't have to say anything. We don't have to talk at all."

He knew what she was offering, even before she tilted her head and touched her lips to his. He wanted it, and her. More than anything, he wanted to steep himself in her until the rest of the world went away.

He took his hands through her hair, letting his fingers toy with those loose, vivid curls. "We haven't come up with those rules."

Her lips curved, slanted over his. "We'll figure them out later."

He murmured his agreement, drawing her closer. "I want you. I need to be with you. I think I'd go crazy if I couldn't be with you tonight."

"I'm here. Right here."

"Bess." His mouth moved from hers to skim along those sharp cheekbones. "I'm in love with you."

She felt her heart stutter. That was the only way she could describe this sensation she'd never experienced before. "Alexi—"

"Don't." He closed his mouth over hers again. "Don't say it. It comes too easy to you. Just come to bed." He buried his face against her neck. "For God's sake, let me take you to bed."

Chapter Eight

Hurt. Oh, she'd read the stories and the poetry, watched the movies. She'd even written the scenes. But she'd never believed that love and pain existed together, could twine into one clenched fist to batter the soul.

Yet his words had hurt her—immeasurably—even as her heart opened to give and accept.

This time it was different. How could she possibly explain that to him, when she was still groping for the answers herself? And what good were words now, when there was so much need?

A touch would be enough, she promised herself as they swayed toward the steps. Tonight would be enough, and tomorrow all the aches would only be memories.

His mouth came back to hers, restless, insistent, as they began the climb. The first helpless sigh caught in her throat as he pulled her close and aroused her unbearably with a long, sumptuous meeting of lips.

Her fingers trembled when she tugged at his jacket. Had they ever trembled for a man before? she wondered. No. And as the leather slid away, leaving her free to grip those magnificent shoulders, she knew that none of this had happened before. Not the trembling, not the raw scrape of nerves, not the sting of bright tears, not the sweet, slow throb of her blood.

This was the first time for so many things.

He didn't know how much longer he could perform the simple act of drawing breath in and out of his lungs. Not when her body was shivering against his. Not when he could hear those small, desperately needy sounds in her throat. The staircase seemed to stretch interminably. With a muffled oath, he swept her up into his arms.

Her eyes met his, and though her heart seemed ready to burst, she managed to smile. She knew he needed smiles tonight. "And I said you weren't romantic."

"I have my moments."

Shaky, she nuzzled her face into the curve of his neck. "I'm awfully glad I'm here for this one."

"Keep it up," he said in a strained voice as she ran nibbling kisses from throat to ear, "and I'll do something really romantic, like falling on my face and dropping you."

"Oh, I trust you, Detective." She caught the lobe of his ear in her teeth and felt the quick jerk of reaction. "Completely."

With his heart roaring in his head, he reached the top. She was teasing his jawline now, making little murmurs of approval as she sampled his flesh. He headed for the first door. "This better be the bed-room."

"Mmm-hmm . . ." While she worked her way to his mouth, her fingers were busy unbuttoning his shirt.

He recognized her scent first. Even as he passed through the doorway, it wrapped its alluring woman's fingers around him. That cheerful, sexy fragrance hung in the air, the result, no doubt, of spilled powder and an unstoppered bottle of perfume. Her clothes were a colorful mess of silk blouses, bright cotton pants, tangled hose. His quick scan passed over a life-size stuffed ostrich, a pair of thriving ficus trees flanking the wide window, and a collection of antique bottles, elegant in jewel colors, before he focused on the bed.

It was a long, wide ocean of cool blue sheets, topped by a lush mountain of vivid-toned pillows. All satins and silks.

Because his mouth was beginning to water, he took one long, slow breath. But the air, so fragrant, burned his lungs. "That looks big enough for six close friends."

"I like a lot of room." Even as his stomach quivered at the images that evoked, she was continuing. "I used to fall out of bed a lot when I was a kid."

"Is that how you broke your nose?"

"No. But I chipped a tooth once."

He set her down beside the bed, pleased that her arms stayed linked around his neck. "I think we can probably keep from falling out of this one. If we work on it."

She raised up on her toes, just a little, just enough to bring them eye-to-eye. "I'm willing to risk it."

Determined to steady himself, he kissed her brow, her cheeks. "Let me take my gun off."

He stripped off the holster, set it on the floor. With fingers that were suddenly numb and awkward, she reached for the buttons of her blazer.

"No." It was that one quick flash of nerves in her eyes that had settled his own. He closed his hands over hers. "Let me." He unfastened buttons, then took his hands slowly up her sides, his thumbs just brushing her breasts. "You're shaking."

"I know."

Watching her, he slid the jacket from her shoulders. "Are you afraid of me?"

"No." She couldn't swallow. "Of this, a little. It's silly."

He toyed with the first button of her blouse, then the second. Her skin quivered as his knuckle skimmed over it. "I like it."

"That's good." She tried to laugh, but only managed one trembling breath. "Because I can't seem to stop."

"There's plenty of time to relax." The blouse slipped away, and desire curled its powerful fist in his stomach. Midnight-blue silk shimmered in the dimming light, gleaming against ivory skin. "There's no hurry."

"I—" Her head fell back as he traced a finger over the silk. Gently, so gently, over the swell of her breasts, as though hers was the first body he'd touched. The only one he wanted to touch. "God, Alexi . . ."

"I've spent a lot of time imagining this. Step out of your shoes," he suggested while he unhooked her slacks. In a daze, she obeyed as the slacks slithered down her legs. "I'm going to spend a lot more time enjoying it. I want all of you." Lazily, testingly, he ran a finger under the lace cut high on her thigh. Ah, the skin there was like rose petals dewed with morning. Her eyes went wide and dark; her body quaked. "All of you," he repeated.

She couldn't move. Every muscle in her body had turned to water. Hot, rushing water. She couldn't speak, not when so many emotions clogged her throat. As she stood swaying, helplessly seduced, he watched her. Touched her. Clever fingers brushing, stroking, exploring. He trailed them up her arms, slid them over her shoulders. Then back to silk, until her body burned like fever.

His eyes never left hers. Even when he kissed her, lightly, tormenting her hungry lips with the barest of tastes, his eyes stayed open and aware.

"You're making me crazy." Her voice hitched out through trembling lips.

"I know. I want to."

He caught her wrists when she reached for him, then ran their tangled fingers over her, so that she felt her own response to him, inside and out, as he touched his mouth to hers again. Patiently, erotically, he deepened the kiss, until her hands went limp and her pulse thundered. Then he brought her hands up, spread them over his chest. Together they spread his open shirt apart. With his mouth still clinging to hers, he tugged it off. His heart gave a quick, hard lurch as her hands, hot and eager, raced over him.

Yanking her close, he took off his shoes. His skin was already damp when he fumbled for the snap of his jeans.

"I want you under me." He tore his mouth from hers to savor her throat. "I want to feel you move under me."

They lowered to the bed, rolled once, then twice, over silk. He used every ounce of control, every degree of will, to keep himself from plunging into her and taking the quick, desperate release his body craved. His mind, his soul, wanted more than that.

She seemed smaller like this. Slighter. It helped him remember that passion could outstrip tenderness. So, while the blood pounded and burned in his veins, he loved her slowly.

She discovered that a woman could drown willingly in sweetness. She knew there was a gun on the floor beside them and that he had used it at least once to kill. But the hands that moved over her were those of a gentle man. One who cared. She rested a palm on his cheek as she floated away on the kiss. One who loved.

Who loved her.

Staggered by the knowledge, she poured everything she had into the kiss, needing to show him that whatever he felt was returned, equally. Then his mouth slid from hers to trail down her throat, over her shoulder. All thought, all reason, skittered away.

In a warm, slippery pool of silk and satin, he showed her what it was to ache for someone. To yearn for the sharp, thin point of pain the poets call ecstasy. Her hips arched under his, desperately offering. But he only continued that tormenting journey over her with teasing lips and gentle hands.

When his tongue flicked under the line of lace that clung tenuously to her breasts, she moaned, pressing an urgent hand to the back of his head. The taste there—honey, dampened by her arousal—nearly unraveled the taut knot of his control. So he pleased them both, closing a greedy mouth over that firm, scented swell.

Gasping out with pleasure, she bucked under him, straining for more, her nails digging heedlessly into his back as she whimpered and struggled for what was just out of reach. Maddened by her response, he brought his mouth to hers again, crushing her lips as he slithered a hand down to cup the heat between her thighs. Prayers and pleas trembled on her tongue, but before she could voice them, he slipped under the silk to stroke.

The unbearable pleasure shattered. Fractured lights, whirling colors, spun behind her eyes to blind her. She heard herself cry out; his name was nearly a sob. Then there was his groan, a sound of sweet satisfaction as her body went limp in release.

Never before. Her hands slid away from him, boneless. Sweet Lord, never like this. She felt weak, wrecked, weepy. As her breath sobbed out, as her eyes fluttered closed, they both knew that her mind, her body, were totally his for the taking.

He'd never felt stronger. Her wild response, her absolute surrender, filled him with a kind of intense power he'd never experienced before. Silk rustled against silk as he drew the teddy down, tossed it aside. Her skin, slick with passion, glowed in the shadows. He touched where he chose, watching, fascinated, as his own hands molded her. Gold against ivory. He tasted wherever he liked, feeling her muscles quiver involuntarily as he traced openmouthed kisses over her rib cage, down to her stomach. Heat to heat.

Then, wanting that instant of sheer pleasure again, he drove her up a second time, shuddering himself as her body convulsed and flowed with the crest of the wave.

At last, unable to wait a moment longer, he slipped inside that hot, moist sheath. Her groan of stunned delight echoed his own.

Slowly, as in a dream, her arms lifted to wrap around him. She rose to meet him, to take him deep. They moved gently at first, treasuring the intimacy, willing to prolong it. But need outpaced them, driving them faster, until, thrust for thrust, they sprinted toward the final crest.

His hand fisted in her hair as the last link of control snapped clean. Her name exploded from his lips like an oath as he emptied himself into her.

She wondered how she could ever have thought herself experienced. While it was true she hadn't been with as many men as some thought, she hadn't come to Alexi an innocent.

Yet things had happened tonight that had never happened before. And, because she was a woman who understood herself well, she knew that nothing she had experienced here would happen again—unless it was with him.

Relaxed now, she rubbed her cheek over his chest, content to remain as she'd been since he rolled over and dragged her across him. Tucked in the cocoon of his arms, she felt as cozy as a cat, and she arched lazily as he ran a hand down her spine.

"Will you tell me again?" she asked.

"What?"

She pressed her lips against him, feeling his heart beating strong and fast beneath them. "What every woman wants to hear."

"I love you." When she lifted her head, he laid a hand gently over her lips. He knew it would hurt to hear her say it, when she didn't mean it as he did.

Suddenly she was glad it was dark, and he couldn't see the smile fade away from her face. "Even after this," she said carefully, "you don't want me to love you back."

More than anything, he thought. More than life. "Let's just leave things as they are." He traced her face with a fingertip, enjoying those odd angles. "Tell me how you broke your nose."

She was silent a moment, gathering her composure. She couldn't offer what he didn't want to take. "Fistfight."

He chuckled and drew her back to cuddle, instinctively soothing the tension out of her. "I should have figured."

She made an effort to relax against him. There was time to convince him. Hadn't he said they had plenty of time? "At boarding school," she added. "I was twelve and homely as a duck. Too skinny, funny hair, dumb face."

"I like your face. And your hair." His hand cupped her breast comfortably. "And your body."

"You didn't know me when I was twelve. When you're odd in any way, you're a target."

"I know."

Interested, she lifted her head again. "Do you?"

"I didn't learn English until I was five. Before my father's business got off the ground, times were rough." He turned his face into her hair to breathe in the scent. "I was this little Ukrainian kid, wearing my brother's hand-me-downs. And back then, Soviets weren't particularly popular with Americans."

"Well, you made such great villains." She kissed his cheek, comforting the small boy he'd been. "It must have been difficult for you."

"I had the family. We had each other. School was a little rugged at first. Name-calling, playground scuffles. Even some of the parents weren't too keen on having their kids play with the Russkie. No point in trying to explain we were Ukrainian." He shifted, tangled his legs with hers. "So, after a few black eyes and bloody noses, I earned a reputation for being tough. After a while, we kind of got absorbed into the neighborhood."

"What neighborhood?"

"Brooklyn. My parents still live there. Same house." With a shake of his head, he drew back. He could make her out now in the dark, could see the way her eyes were smiling at him. "How come we're talking about me, when I asked you about your nose?"

"I like hearing it."

"There was a fistfight," he said, prompting her.

Bess sighed. "One of those girl cliques," she began. "You know the type. The cool kids, all hair and teeth and attitude. I was the nerd they liked to pick on."

"You were never a nerd."

"I was a *champion* nerd. Gawky, top of the class academically, socially inept."

"You?"

There was such pure disbelief in the tone, she laughed. "Which of those descriptions don't you buy, Alexi?"

He considered a moment. "Any of them."

"I guess I'm two-thirds flattered and one-third insulted. I was tall for my age and skinny. A very late bloomer in the bosom and hips department."

"You might have bloomed slow," he began, proving his point with a sweep of his hand, "but you bloomed very well."

"Thank you. My mind, however, had developed quite nicely. Straight *A*'s."

"No kidding?" He grinned in the dark. "And you were the kid who always trashed the grading curve for the rest of us."

"That's the idea. Added to that, I was more comfortable with a book, or thinking, than I was tittering. Young girls do a lot of tittering. Because I was hardheaded, I automatically took a dislike to anything that was popular or fashionable at the time. As a result, I took a lot of flak. Bess the Mess, that sort of thing."

She paused long enough to shift some pillows. "Anyway, we had this history exam coming up. One of the cool kids—her name was Dawn Gallagher... Heart-shaped face, perfect features, long, flowing blond hair. You get the picture."

"Prom-queen type."

"Exactly. She was flunking big-time and wanted me to let her copy from my paper. She'd made my life adolescent hell, and she figured if she was nice to me for a couple of days, let me stand within five feet of her, maybe sit at the same lunch table, I'd be so grateful, I'd let her."

"But you hung tough."

"I don't cheat for anybody. The upshot was, she flunked the exam, and her parents were called to the school for a conference. Dawn retaliated by pinching me whenever I got too close, getting into my room and breaking my things, stealing my books. Small-time terrorism. One day on the basketball court—''

''You shot hoop?''

''Team captain. I was an athletic nerd,'' she explained. ''Anyway, she tripped me. If that wasn't bad enough, she had a few friends on the other team. They elbowed the hell out of me during the game. I had bruises everywhere.''

An immediate flood of resentment had him tightening his hold. ''Little bitches.''

Pleased with the support, she cuddled closer. ''It was an epiphany for me. Suddenly I saw that pacifism, while morally sound, could get you trampled into dust. I waited for Dawn outside the science lab one day. We started out with words—I've always been good at them. We progressed to pushing and shoving and drew quite a crowd. She swung first. I didn't expect it, and she bopped me right on the nose. Let me tell you, Detective, pain can be a great motivator.''

''Separates the nerds from the toughs.''

''You got it. It took three of them to pull me off her, but before they did, I'd blackened her baby-blues, split her Cupid's-bow mouth and loosened several of her pearly-whites.''

''Good for you, McNee.''

''It was good,'' she said with a sigh. ''In fact, it felt so good, I've had to be careful with my temper ever since. I didn't just want to hurt her, you see. I wanted to mangle her.''

He took her hand, curled it into a fist and raised it to his lips. ''I'll have to watch my step. Did you take much heat?''

"We both got suspended. My parents were appalled and embarrassed enough by my behavior to cancel my summer plans and switch me to another school."

"But—" He cut himself off. Not every family was as supportive as his.

"It was the best thing that could have happened to me," she told him. "I started off with a clean slate. I was still ugly, but I knew how to handle myself."

Even if she didn't realize she was carrying around some emotional scars, he did. He rolled over her, cupping her face in his hands. "Listen, McNee, you're beautiful."

Amused, she grinned. "Sure I am."

He didn't smile. In the dim light, his eyes were very intense. "I said, you're beautiful. Why else haven't I been able to get you out of my mind since the first time I saw you?"

"Intriguing," she corrected. "Unusual."

"Gorgeous," he murmured, and watched her blink in surprise. "Ivory for skin, fire for hair, jade for eyes. And these." He traced a fingertip over a sprinkling of freckles. "Gold dust."

"You've already gotten me into bed, Alexi," she said lightly. She had to speak lightly, or she'd humiliate herself with tears. "But the flattery is appreciated." With a grin, she linked her arms around his neck. "But haven't you heard the one about actions speaking louder than words?"

He arched a brow. "If you insist."

"Oh, I do," she murmured, as his mouth came down to hers. "I absolutely do."

* * *

With her bag slapping hard against her hip, Bess raced into the office, ten minutes late. "I have a good excuse," she called to Lori.

Her perpetually prompt partner was standing by the coffeepot, her back to the door. "It's all right. I'm running behind myself."

"You?" Bess dropped her bag, stretched her shoulders. She might have skipped her workout that morning, but she was feeling as limber as a snake. "What is it, a national holiday?" She crossed to the pot herself, chattering as she poured a cup. "Well, I'd save my excuse for another time, but I can hardly stand not to tell you." She lifted shining eyes, then stopped after one look at Lori's face. "What is it, honey?"

"It's nothing." After giving herself a shake, Lori sipped her coffee. "It's just that Steven caught me on my way in."

"Did he say something to upset you?"

"He said he loved me." She pressed her lips together. She'd be damned if she'd cry over him again. "The sonofabitch."

"Let's sit down." Bess curled a comforting arm around Lori's shoulder. "You might not want to hear this, but I think he means it."

"He doesn't even know what it means." Furious, Lori dashed one rogue tear away. "I'm not going to let him do this to me again. Get me believing, get me all churned up, just so he can back off when things get serious. Let him have the fantasy life. I've got reality."

Because she'd been waiting for an opening just like this, Bess crouched down in front of her. "Which is?"

"A job, paying your bills—"

"Boring," Bess finished, and Lori's brimming eyes flashed.

"Then I'm boring."

"No, you're not." Sighing, Bess set her coffee aside and took one of Lori's hands. "Maybe you're afraid to take risks, but that doesn't make you boring. And I know you want more out of life than a job and a good credit rating."

"What's wrong with those things?"

"Nothing, as long as that's not all you have. Lori, I know you're still in love with him."

"That's my problem."

"His, too. He's miserable without you."

Suddenly weary, Lori rubbed her fingers between her brows. "He's the one who broke things off. He said he didn't want complications, a long-term commitment."

"He was wrong. I'd bet the bank that he knows he's wrong. Why don't you just talk to him?"

"I don't know if I can." She squeezed her eyes tight. "It hurts."

An odd light flickered in Bess's eyes. "Is that how you know it's real? When it hurts?"

"It's one of the top symptoms." She opened her eyes again. This time, there was a trace of hope mixed with the tears. "Do you really think he's unhappy?"

"I know he is. Just talk, Lori. Hear each other out."

"Maybe." She gave Bess's hand a quick squeeze, then reached for her coffee again. "I wasn't going to dump this on you first thing."

"What are pals for?"

"Well, pal, we'd better get to work, or a lot of people will be out of a job."

"Great. I've been playing with the dialogue in that scene between Storm and Jade. We want to bump up the sexual tension."

Lori was already nodding and booting up the computer. "You're the dialogue champ," she began, then glanced up. "So why were you late?"

"It's not important. We've got them running into each other at the station house. The long look first, then—"

"Bess, you're only making me more curious. Get it out of the way, or I won't be able to work."

"Okay." She was all but bursting to tell, in any case. "I was with Alexi."

"I thought that was yesterday."

"It was." Bess's smile spread. "And last night. And this morning. Oh, Lori, it's incredible. I've never felt this way about anyone."

"Right." She started to pick up her reading glasses, then looked up again. For a moment, she did nothing but study Bess's face. "Say that again."

"I've never felt this way about anyone."

"Good grief." On a quick huff of breath, Lori sat back. "I think you mean it."

"It's different." With a half laugh, Bess pressed a hand to her cheek. "It's scary, and it hurts, and sometimes I look at him and I can't even breathe. I'm so afraid he might take a good look at me and realize his mistake." She let her hand drop away. "It's supposed to be easy."

"No." Slowly Lori shook her head. "That was always *your* mistake. It's supposed to be hard, and scary and real."

"There's this clutching around my heart."

"Yeah."

"And ... and ..." Frustrated, Bess turned, scooting around a chair so that she could pace the length of the table. "And my stomach's all tied up in knots one minute. The next I feel so happy I can hardly bear it. When we were together last night ..." No way to describe it, she thought. No possible way. "Lori, I swear, no one's ever made me feel like that. And this morning, when I woke up beside him, I didn't know whether to laugh or cry."

Lori rose, held out a hand. "Congratulations, McNee. You've finally made it."

"Looks that way." With a laugh, she threw her arms around Lori and squeezed. "Why didn't you ever tell me how it feels?"

"It's something you have to experience firsthand. How about him?"

"He loves me." She felt foolish and weepy. Digging through her bag she found a tattered tissue. "He told me. He looked at me, and he told me. But—"

"Oh-oh."

"He doesn't want me to tell him how I feel." Hissing a breath through her teeth, she pressed a hand to her stomach. "Oh, God, it hurts. It hurts everywhere when I realize he doesn't trust me enough. He thinks it's like all the other times. Why shouldn't he? But I want him to know it's not—and I don't know how."

"He only has to look at you."

"It's not enough." Calmer now, Bess blew her nose. "Everything's different this time. I guess I have to prove myself. I do love him, Lori."

"I can see that. I wasn't sure I ever would." Touched, she lifted a hand to Bess's hair. "You could take your own advice, and talk to him."

"We have talked. But he doesn't want to hear this, at least not yet. He wants things to stay as they are."

Lori lifted her brows. "What do you want?"

"For him to be happy." She chuckled and stuffed the mangled tissue back in her purse. "That makes me sound like a wimp. You know I'm not."

"Who knows you better? It only makes you sound like a woman in the first dizzy stages of love."

Bess gave her a watery smile. "Does it get worse or better?"

"Both."

"That's good news. Well, while it's getting worse and better, I'll have time to show him how I feel." She picked up her coffee, then set it aside again. "Lori, there's one more thing."

"What could be bigger?" Lori demanded.

"Alexi wants me to have dinner with his family on Sunday."

After a quick gurgle of laughter, Lori's eyes widened. "He's taking you home to Mother?"

"And Father," Bess put in. "And brothers and sisters and nieces and nephews. A couple times a month they have a big family dinner on Sunday."

"Obviously the man is crazy about you."

"He is. I know he is." Then she shut her eyes and dropped into a chair. "His family is enormously important to him. You can hear it every time he mentions one of them." She grabbed another tissue and began to tear it to shreds. "I want to meet them. Really. But what if they don't like me?"

"You have got it bad. Take it from me, you just be the Bess McNee we all know and love, and they'll be crazy about you, too."

"But what if—"

"What if you pull yourself together?" This time Lori picked up her glasses, perched them on her nose. "Put some of this angst into Storm and Jade's heartbreak. Millions of viewers will thank you."

After a deep breath, Bess nodded. "Okay, okay. That might work. And if we don't get the morning session out of the way, we won't be ready when Rosalie comes in at noon for a consulting session."

"Your deal, sister." Frowning, Lori gestured with a pencil. "That particular lady makes me nervous."

"Don't worry about Rosalie. I know what I'm doing."

"How many times have I heard that?"

But Bess only smiled and let her mind drift. "Okay. Storm and Jade." She closed her eyes, envisioned the scene. "So, they run into each other at the station..."

Chapter Nine

"And then," Bess continued as she zipped through traffic, "Jade turns back, devastated, and says, 'But what you want isn't always what you need.' Music swells, fade out."

"It's not that I'm not fascinated by the twists and turns of those people in Holbrook..."

"Millbrook."

"Right." Alex winced as she cut off a sedan. "I just wish you'd watch the road. It would be really embarrassing if you got a ticket while I was in the car with you."

"I'm not speeding." Frowning, she glanced down at her speedometer. "Hardly."

She handled the five-speed like a seasoned veteran of the Indianapolis 500, Alex thought. And at the moment she was treating the other, innocent drivers on the road like competitors. "Maybe you could find a home in one lane and stay there."

"Killjoy." But she did as he asked. "I hardly ever get to drive. I love it."

He had to smile. The wind whipping in through the open sunroof was blowing her hair everywhere. "I'd never have guessed."

"The last time I had a chance was when L.D. and I went to some fancy do on Long Island." She checked her mirror and, unable to resist, shot into the next lane. "One trip with me and he insisted on taking his car and driver every damn place." She sent Alex a smile, then sobered instantly when she saw his expression. "I'm sorry."

"For what?"

"For bringing him up."

"I didn't say anything."

No, he hadn't said anything, she admitted. A man didn't have to say a word when his eyes could go that cold. Her hands tightened on the wheel. Now she stared straight ahead.

"He was a friend, Alexi. That's all he ever was. I didn't..." She took a long, careful breath. "I never slept with him."

"I didn't ask one way or the other," he said coolly.

"Maybe you should. One minute you want to know all there is about me, and the next you don't. I think—"

"I think you're driving too fast again." He reached over and brushed his knuckles down her cheek. "And you should relax. Okay?"

"Okay." But her fingers remained tight on the wheel. "I'd like—sometime—for us to talk about it."

"Sometime." Damn it, didn't she realize he didn't want to talk about the other men who'd been part of her life? He didn't want to think about them. Especially now, now that he was in love, and he knew what it was like to be with her.

He knew the sound of that little sigh she made when she turned toward him in the night. The way her eyes stayed unfocused and heavy, long after she awakened in the morning. He knew she liked her showers too hot and too long. And that she smelled so good because she rubbed some fragrant cream all over before she'd even dried off.

She was always losing things. An earring, a scribbled note, money. She never counted her change, and she always overtipped.

He knew those things, was coming to treasure them. Why should he talk about other men who had come to know them?

"Turn here."

"Hmm?"

"I said turn..." He trailed off with a huff of breath as she breezed by the exit. "Okay, take the next one, and we'll double back."

"The next what?"

"Turn, McNee." He reached over and gave her hair a quick tug. "Take the next turn, which means you have to get over in the right lane."

"Oh." She did, punching the gas and handily cutting off another car. At the rude blast of its horn, she only lifted a hand and waved.

"He wasn't being friendly," Alex pointed out—after he took his hands from in front of his eyes.

"I know. But that's no reason for me to be rude, too." "You've got good ears."

"Some people consider cutting off another driver rude."

"No. That's an adventure."

Somehow they made it without mishap. But the moment she'd squeezed into a parking place two doors down from his parents' row house, he held out his hand. "Keys."

Sulking, she jingled them in her hand. "I didn't get a ticket."

"Probably because there wasn't a traffic cop brave enough to pull you over. Let's have them, McNee. I've had enough adventure for one day."

"You just want to drive." Her eyes narrowed suspiciously. "It's a man thing."

"It's a survival thing." He plucked them from her hand. "I just want to live." Not that he was going to object to handling the natty little Mercedes. But he decided against bringing that up as they climbed out of opposite doors.

"Pretty neighborhood," she commented, taking in the trees and freshly painted house trim and flowering plants, the scatter of kids riding over the uneven sidewalk on bikes and skateboards.

A few of them called out to Alex. Bess found herself being given the once-over by a group of teenage boys before they sent hoots and whistles and thumbs-up signs in Alex's direction.

"Ah, the first stamp of approval." But she rubbed her damp palm surreptitiously against her skirt before taking his hand. "Did you used to ride bikes along the sidewalk?"

"Sure."

Battling nerves, she strolled with him toward the house. "And sit on the curb in the summer and lie about girls?"

"I didn't have to lie," he told her with a wicked grin. He glanced up the steps as the door opened and Mikhail came out, Griff on his hip.

"You're late again." He started down, jiggling Griff.

"She missed the turn."

"He's always late." Mikhail smiled. "You're Bess."

"Yes. Hello." She held out a hand and found that his was hard as rock. Griff had already leaned over to give Alex a kiss, and now, still puckered, he leaned toward Bess. Laughing, she pressed her mouth to his. "And hello to you, too, handsome."

"Griff likes the ladies," Mikhail told her. "Takes after his uncle."

"Don't start," Alex muttered.

Mikhail ignored him and continued to study Bess until she was fighting the need to squirm. "Do I have dirt on my face, or what?"

"No, sorry." He shifted his gaze to his brother. "You're improving, Alexi," he said in Ukrainian. "This one is well worth a few sweaty mornings in the gym."

"*Tak*." He skimmed a hand down to the nape of Bess's neck. "If you tell her about that, I'll strangle you in your sleep."

Mikhail's grin flashed. The resemblance was startling, Bess thought. Those wild, dark looks, that simmering sexuality. And the child had the looks, as well, she realized. Lord help the women of the twenty-first century.

"Guy talk?" she asked.

"Bad manners," Mikhail said apologetically, deciding he liked not only her unusual looks, but the intelligence in her eyes, as well. Yes, indeed, he thought, Alex was definitely improving. "I was complimenting my brother on his taste. Take her in, Alex. Griff wants to watch the kids ride awhile."

"Sydney?" he asked as he mounted the steps.

"She's here, but she's tired."

"She works too hard."

"There is that." The grin spread again. "And she's pregnant."

Alex stopped, turned. "Yeah?" He went down the steps again to catch Mikhail and Griff in a bear hug. "It's good?"

"It's great. We want our children close, our family big."

"You're off to the right start." He grabbed Bess's hand as Mikhail lifted Griff onto his shoulders and crossed the street. Griff was clapping his hands and shouting toddler gibberish to the other kids. "I'm still trying to get used to him being a papa, and now he's going to have another."

She'd forgotten her nerves. Perhaps the child's sweet, unaffected kiss had done it. She slipped an arm around Alex's waist. "Come on, Uncle Alex. I want to meet the rest of them."

"They're loud," he warned as they started back up the door.

"I like loud."

"They can be nosy."

"So can I."

At the door, he took both of her hands. He'd brought women into his home before, but it had never been important. This was vital. "I love you, Bess."

Before she could speak, he kissed her, then pushed open the door.

They certainly were loud, Bess discovered. No one seemed to mind if everyone talked at once, or if the big, droopy-eared dog barked and raced around the living room to hide behind chairs. And they were nosy, though they were charming with it. She'd hardly had a chance to get her bearings before she was sitting next to Alex's father, Yuri, and being cagily interrogated.

"So you write stories for TV." He nodded his big, shaggy head approvingly. "You have brains."

"A few." She smiled up at Zack when he offered her a glass of wine.

"Rachel says more than a few." He sent his wife a wink as she sat with her hands folded over her enormous belly. "She's been watching your show."

"Oh, yeah?"

"I admit I was curious." Rachel wanted to shift to get comfortable, but she knew it was useless. "After we met, I taped it a couple of times. Then, when I gave in to Zack's hounding me about taking maternity leave, I realized how easy it is to get hooked. I'm not sure I've got all the characters straight yet, but it's amazingly entertaining. Nick's caught it with me." She glanced at her brother-in-law.

To his credit, Nick didn't blush, but he did squirm. "I was just keeping you company." He might have come a long way from trying to prove his manhood with gangs like the Cobras, but even at nearly twenty-one, he wasn't quite secure enough to admit he'd gotten caught up in the "Secret Sins" of Millbrook. He shrugged, shook back his shaggy blond hair, then caught the quick grins of his family. "It wasn't like I was really watching.'' His green eyes glinted with humor. ''Except for the babes.''

''That's what they all say.'' Bess smiled back, enjoying him. Too bad he wasn't an actor, she thought. Those brooding good looks—tough, with just a hint of vulnerability beneath—would shine on-screen. ''So, who's your type, Nick? LuAnne, our sensitive ingenue with the big, weepy eyes, who suffers in silence, or the scheming Brooke, who uses her sexuality to destroy any man who crosses her?''

Considering, he ran his tongue around his teeth. ''Actually, I go for Jade. I've got this thing for older women.''

Zack caught him in a headlock.

''Hey.'' Nick laughed, not bothering to try to free himself. ''We're having a conversation here. I'm trying to make time with Alex's lady.''

''Kill him in the other room, will you?'' Alex said easily. ''We have to eat in here.''

''I watch your show many times,'' Nadia said as she popped in from the kitchen. Alex's mother's handsome face was flushed pink from oven heat. ''I like it.''

''Well, that Vicki's not hard to watch.'' Zack stood behind his wife now, rubbing her shoulders.

''Men always go for the cheap floozies,'' Rachel put in. ''How about you, Alex? Caught any 'Secret Sins'?''

''No.'' Not that he'd admit. ''McNee keeps me up on what's happening in Millbrook.''

''It must be hard.'' Sydney, looking pale but blissfully relaxed in her corner of the couch, sipped her ginger ale. ''The pace.''

''It's murder.'' Bess grinned. ''I love it.''

"So, how is it you meet Alexi?" Yuri asked.

"He arrested me."

There was a moment of silence, while Alex aimed a killing look at Bess. Then a burst of laughter that sent the dog careening around the room again.

"Did I miss a joke?" Mikhail demanded as he swung through the door with Griff.

"No." Rachel chuckled again while her brother sat on the arm of the couch, beside his wife. "But I have a feeling it's going to be a good one. Come on, Bess, this I have to hear."

She told them, while Alex interrupted a half-dozen times to disagree or correct or put in his own perspective. Even as they sat at the big old table to enjoy Nadia's pot roast, they were shouting with laughter or calling out questions.

"He put you in a cell, but you still go out with him." This from Mikhail.

"Well." Bess ran her tongue over her teeth. "He is kind of cute."

With a hearty laugh, Yuri slapped his son on the back. "The ladies, they always say so."

Alex scooped up potatoes. "Thanks, Papa."

"Is good to be attractive to women." He wiggled his brows at his wife. "Then, when you pick one, she is helpless to resist."

"I picked you," Nadia told him, passing biscuits to Nick. "You were very slow. Like a bear with, ah..." She struggled for the right word. "Soft brains." She ignored Yuri's snort of objection. "He did not come to court me. So I courted him."

"Every time I turn, there she is. In my way." When he looked at his wife, Bess saw memories and more in his eyes. "There was no prettier girl in the village than Nadia. Then she was mine."

"I liked your big hands and shy eyes," she told him. Her smile was quick and lovely. "Soon you were not so shy. But my boys," she added, turning the smile on Bess, "they were never shy with the girls."

"Why waste time?" On impulse, Alex put a hand on Bess's cheek and turned her face to his. Her smile was puzzled. Then surprise shot into her eyes as he covered her mouth with his. Not a quick, friendly kiss, this, but a searing one that made her head buzz.

She had no way of knowing that he'd never kissed a woman not of his family at his mother's table. Nor that by doing so, he was telling those he loved that this was *the* woman.

As the table erupted with applause, Bess cleared her throat. "No," she managed. "Not a bit shy."

Nadia blinked back tears and raised her glass. She understood what her son had told her and felt the bittersweet pleasure that came from knowing the last of her children had given his heart. "Welcome," she said to Bess.

A little confused, Bess reached for her glass as all the others were lifted. "Thank you." She sipped, relieved when the chattering started again.

How easy to fall in love with them, she realized. All of them were so warm, so open, so comfortable with each other. Her parents would never have had such a sweetly intimate conversation at the table. Nor had they ever embraced her with the verve and passion both Yuri and Nadia showed their children.

Was this what she'd been missing all of those years? Bess wondered. Had lacking something like this caused her to be so socially clumsy as a child, and, making up for it, so socially active as an adult?

Still, what she had had, and what she hadn't, had forged her into what she was, so she couldn't regret it. Well, perhaps a little, she mused, falling unknowingly into the family tradition by sneaking the dog bits of food under the table. It was hard not to regret it a little when you saw how lovely it could be to be part of such a solid whole.

Absorbing everything, she glanced around the table. And found Mikhail's eyes on her. This time she smiled. ''You're doing it again,'' she told him.

''Yes. I want to carve you.''

''I beg your pardon?''

''Your face.'' He reached out to take it in his hand. The conversation continued around them, as if he handled women at the dinner table regularly. ''Very fascinating. Mahogany would be best.''

Amused, she sat patiently while he turned her face this way and that. ''Is this a joke?''

''Mikhail never jokes about his work,'' Sydney commented, coaxing one more green bean into her son. ''I'm just surprised it's taken him so long to demand you sit for him.''

''Sit?'' She shook her head, and then her eyes widened as it all came together. ''Oh, of course. Stanislaski. The artist. I've seen your work. Lusted after it, actually.''

''You will sit for me, and I'll give you a piece. You'll choose it.''

''I could hardly turn down an offer like that.''

''Good.'' Satisfied, he went back to his meal. ''She's very beautiful,'' he said to Alex, in such an offhand way that Bess laughed.

"I'd say that Stanislaski taste runs to the odd, but your wife proves me wrong."

Mikhail brushed a hand over Sydney's halo of auburn hair, stroked a finger down her classically lovely face. "There are different kinds of beauty. You'll come to the studio next week."

"Don't bother to argue." Sydney caught Mikhail's hand, squeezed it. "It won't do you a bit of good."

At the other end of the table, Rachel winced. Nadia leaned closer, spoke gently. "How far apart?"

Rachel gave a little sigh. "Eight, ten minutes. They're very mild yet."

"What's mild?" Zack glanced at her, and then his mouth all but dropped to his knees. "Oh, God, now? *Now?*"

"Not this very minute." She would be calm, Rachel told herself and took a deep, cleansing breath to prove it. "I think you have time for some of Mama's cream cake."

"She's in labor." He gaped across the table at his equally panicked brother.

"We're not ready here." Nick stumbled to his feet. "We're ready back at home. I'm supposed to call the doctor, but I don't have the number."

"Mama does," Rachel assured her husband's younger brother. Then she lifted a hand to her husband's. "Take it easy, Muldoon. There's plenty of time."

"Time, hell. We're going now. Shouldn't we go now?" Zack demanded of Nadia.

She smiled and nodded. "It would be best for you, Zack."

"But, Mama—"

Rachel's protest was cut off by Nadia's gentle flow of Ukrainian, the gist of which had a great deal to do with placating frightened husbands.

"She should put her feet up," Mikhail announced. "This helped you, yes?"

"Yes," Sydney agreed. "But I think we should wait until she gets to the hospital."

"Nine-one-one." Alex shoved away from the table and sprang to his feet. "I'll call."

"Oh, sit down." Rachel waved an annoyed hand at him. "I don't need a cop."

"An ambulance," he insisted.

"I'm not sick, I'm in labor."

"I take her in the truck." Yuri was already up, prepared to lift his baby girl into his big arms. "We get there very fast."

While the men began to argue in a mixture of languages, Nadia rose quietly and went into the kitchen to call Rachel's obstetrician.

"I've already been through this," Mikhail was saying to Alex. "I know how to handle it."

"Ha." Their father pushed them both aside and pounded a fist on his broad chest. "Me, four times. You know nothing."

"We don't have the tape recorder or the music." Nick ran a hand through his flow of sandy hair. He was desperately afraid he'd be sick. Though no one was listening to him, he continued to babble. "The video camera. We've got to get the video camera."

"Honey, you want some water? You want some juice?" When she yelped, he turned dead white. "Another one? It hasn't been ten minutes, has it?"

"You're breaking my hand." Rachel shook it free and sent a pleading look to Sydney.

"Okay, guys, back off." The steel under velvet that made Sydney a successful businesswoman snapped into her voice. "Alex, go upstairs and get your sister a pillow for the ride. Yuri, go start the truck. That's a very good idea. Nick, you, Mikhail and Griff go back to your apartment and get what Rachel needs. We'll meet you at the hospital."

"How do you get there?" Mikhail demanded.

"I have a car." Bess was watching the family drama with fascinated eyes. "We can fit three in a pinch."

"Wonderful." Dispersing the troops with all the flair of a general, Sydney gave her husband a kiss and a shove. "Get going. Zack and Nadia will ride with Yuri and Rachel. I'll go with Alex and Bess."

As the next contraction hit, Rachel began to breathe slowly, steadily. "Sorry," she said to Bess in between breaths, "to put you out."

"No problem." She had to bite her tongue to prevent herself asking what it felt like to go into labor at a family dinner. There'd be time for that later.

"I called the doctor, and Natasha." Nadia came back into the room, pleased that Sydney had organized the troops. "Natasha and her family are coming."

"We should go." Zack helped Rachel to her feet and swallowed hard. "Shouldn't we go?"

By the time they arrived at the hospital, Sydney and Bess were the best of friends. It was difficult to be otherwise, when they'd been crammed together in one seat while Alex drove like a madman back to Manhattan.

They talked about clothes, a few mutual friends they'd discovered, and the Stanislaski men. Sydney agreed that it was very forbearing of Bess not to mention the quality of Alex's driving, after he'd been so critical of hers.

By the time they found their way to the maternity level, Rachel was already settled in a birthing room, Zack had gotten over the first stages of panic, and Yuri was patting a pocket full of cigars.

"She's in the early stages," Nadia explained to them in the corridor. "Company is good for her."

Alex strode straight through the door, but Bess hung back. "I don't want to intrude," she said to Nadia.

"This is not intrusion. This is family." Nadia cocked her head. "Are you uneasy with childbirth?"

"Oh, no. I couldn't be, after I've written so many."

Alex poked his head back out. "How'd you research that, McNee?"

"I did rounds with an obstetrician." Her dimple winked out. "And found a few mothers-to-be who didn't object to having me hang around during labor and delivery. Have you ever seen one?"

"No." His eyes changed. Just like a man. "They, ah, show us films, just in case, but I've never been at ground zero."

"It's pretty great." She laughed, perfectly able to read his thoughts. "Don't worry. I'll hold your hand."

They passed the time in the big, airy birthing room telling stories, giving advice, joking with Zack once Mikhail and Nick arrived with Rachel's things. Griff was happily settled in with Zack's cook, Rio, so there was little to do but wait.

When Rachel felt like walking, they took turns leading her around the corridors, rubbing her back, making small talk to take her mind off the discomfort between contractions.

"I can see your mind working," Alex murmured to Bess. "'How can I use this?'"

"It's ingrained." She murmured her thanks when he passed her his cold drink. "Your family," she said, glancing around the room. "I've never known anyone like them. My parents—they'd be appalled to be expected to take part in something like this."

"It's our baby, too."

She smiled and lifted a hand to his cheek. "That's what I mean. You're all very special."

"I'm glad you're here." As he leaned over to kiss her, Yuri slapped him on the back.

"Now all my children make babies but you." He wiggled his brows at Bess. "You start soon, yes?"

"Papa..." Not sure how to take Bess's chuckle, Alex rose and spoke, firmly and quietly, in his mother tongue. "When I decide to make babies, I'll let you know."

"What decide?" Yuri gestured toward Bess. "She's the one you want, isn't she?"

"Yes."

Now Yuri gestured expansively with both hands. "Then?"

"I have my reasons for waiting. They're my reasons."

Though the shake of Yuri's head was a gesture of sadness, there was a twinkle in his eye. "How is it all my children are so stubborn?"

"How is it my papa is so nosy?"

With a laugh, Yuri embraced Alex and kissed both his cheeks. "Go take this pretty girl for a walk, steal some kisses. Your sister will be some time yet."

"That's advice I'll take." He reached for Bess's hand and pulled her to her feet. "Come on, let's get some air."

"Alexi." Bess had to quicken her pace to keep up with him. "Don't be angry with him. He didn't mean to embarrass you."

"Yes, he did, but I'm not angry with him."

"What were you two rattling on about?"

He punched the button for the elevator. "You know, I don't think I'll teach you any Ukrainian. It comes in too handy."

"But it's—"

"Rude," he finished for her, grinning. "I know."

By the time they came back again, Alex had taken his father's advice to heart. Bess's head was still spinning when they walked past the waiting room. It was Alex who spotted Nick, pacing and smoking in the smoking lounge like the cliché expectant daddy.

"How's it going, kid?"

"It's been an awfully long time." Nick's hand shook a bit as he lifted the cigarette to his lips. "I mean, Sydney was only in a couple of hours for Griff. It's getting really intense, and Rachel kicked me and the camera out. How come they don't do something?"

"I don't know a lot about it," Alex mused. "But I think babies come when they're ready."

"It's only been a little more than six hours." Bess moved in to soothe, touched that Nick should have such deep concern for his sister-in-law.

"Feels like six days," Zack commented as he staggered in. He plucked the cigarette from Nick's hand and took a deep drag. "She's swearing at me. I know what some of those names are now, even if they aren't in English.''

''That's a good sign,'' Bess assured him. ''It means things are moving along.''

''She swore at the doctor, too.'' With a sigh, he passed the cigarette back to Nick. ''But she didn't take a swing at *him*.''

''If she missed,'' Alex commented, ''she must be in really bad shape.''

Wincing, Zack rubbed his shoulder. ''She didn't. I'd better get back.''

''Let's go give him some support,'' Alex began, but then he spotted a woman rushing off the elevator. ''Tash!''

''Oh, Alex!''

Bess watched the woman fly into the waiting room, Gypsy hair flowing. There was concern in her eyes and laughter on her lips as she swung into Alex's arms.

''Alexi, how is Rachel?''

''Swearing at her doctor and punching Zack.''

''Ah.'' She relaxed instantly. ''That's good. Nick.'' She held out a hand for his. ''Don't look so worried. Your niece or nephew will be along soon. Spence is parking the car. We were going to leave the children, but they were so disappointed, we brought them. Freddie's looking forward to seeing you.''

Nick brightened a bit. ''How's she doing?''

''She's taller than me now, and so pretty. Alex, where's Rachel?''

''I'll take you. Oh, this is Bess.''

''Bess?'' Natasha turned, one hand still on her brother's arm. Of course, she'd heard about Bess. West Virginia might be a fair distance from New York, but family business traveled fast on phone wires. "I'm sorry. I didn't realize."

"That's all right. You've got a lot on your mind." And then Bess said the first thing that came to hers. "What fabulous genes you all have."

Natasha's brows lifted. Then, below them, her eyes lit with laughter. "Rachel said I would like you. I hope we have time to talk before we leave town. I'm sorry to rush off."

"Don't worry about it. I think Nick and I'll go to the cafeteria, rustle up some food for this group."

Three hours later, Bess had delivered sandwiches and coffee, bounced Natasha's youngest daughter, Katie, on her knee and introduced herself to Spence Kimball and helped him entertain his very cranky son. She'd met Freddie and noted that the pretty, pixielike teenager was deep in puppy love with Nick.

As time dragged on, she added her support when Mikhail pressured his very tired wife to rest in the waiting room, took a few minutes to interrogate some nurses to help her beef up some hospital scenes and soothed Alex's nerves as his sister's labor reached the final stages.

"It won't be much longer."

"That's what they said an hour ago."

They were standing in the waiting room. Alex refused to sit. After a yawn and a good stretch, Bess wrapped her arms around him.

"She's fully dilated, and the baby was crowning. The last glance I had of the fetal monitor showed a really strong heartbeat. A fast one. I think it's a girl."

"How do you know so much?"

"Research." She settled her head on his shoulder. "I was figuring earlier that I've delivered twelve babies, including one set of twins. In a matter of speaking."

When her voice slurred, he tipped up her chin. "You're asleep on your feet, McNee. I should have sent you home."

"You couldn't have pried me away."

No, that was true, he realized. It was just one more aspect to her beauty. "I owe you."

"Then pay up." She lifted her mouth, sighing into the kiss.

"Mama." Though he'd enjoyed watching his brother, Mikhail shot to his feet when he spotted his parents in the doorway.

"We have a new member of the family." There were tears in Nadia's eyes and in Yuri's as he stood with his arm tight around his wife.

"What is it?" Nick and Alex demanded together.

"You will come see. They bring the baby to the glass in a moment."

"Rachel is resting." Yuri dashed away a tear. "You will kiss her good night soon."

They trooped out together, to wait by the nursery window for the first glimpse.

"I'm an uncle," Nick said to Freddie. The girl's cheeks turned pink as he gave her a hard hug. "Hey, there's Zack." He kept his arm around her as his brother walked forward, holding a tiny bundle. The bundle was squalling, and Zack was grinning from ear to ear.

He held the baby up. Atop the curling black hair was a bright pink bow.

"It's a girl," Alex murmured, and held Bess hard against him. "She's beautiful."

"Man" was the best Nick could do. "Oh, man." Overcome for a moment, he glanced down and found himself looking at Freddie, who was still tucked under his arm. He drew back, brushed a fingertip along her cheek and caught a tear on the tip. "What's this?"

"It's just so sweet." Freddie's eyelashes were spiky and her eyes swam as she looked up at him. He thought for a moment—an uncomfortable moment— that it would be easy to drown in those eyes.

"Yeah, it's great." He let out a careful breath. She was his cousin, he reminded himself. Well, a kind of cousin. And she was hardly more than a kid. "I, ah, don't have a handkerchief or anything."

"It's all right." Freddie felt a drop roll down her cheek, but she didn't mind. After all, these were the very best kind of tears. "Do *you* ever think about having babies?" she asked with disarming candor.

"Having—" Nick would have stepped back then, way back, but the family was crowding him in. "No," he said firmly, and made himself look away from her damp, glowing face. "No way."

"I do." She sighed and let her head rest against his arm.

Mikhail was whispering something to Sydney that had her nodding and wiping away tears. Behind Freddie, Natasha shifted Katie in her arms and turned to her husband. He had one hand on Freddie's shoulder, and his sleeping son lay curved on his own.

"Every one is a miracle."

He bent his head to kiss her damp cheeks. "Just say the word anytime you decide you'd like another miracle of our own."

"I am a man blessed." Yuri grabbed the closest body. It happened to be Bess's, and she found herself whirled in a circle. "Two grandsons. Now three granddaughters." He tossed Bess up. She came down laughing, gripping his shoulders.

"Congratulations." She pleased him enormously by kissing him firmly on the mouth. "Grandpapa."

"It's a good day." He reached in his pocket. "Have a cigar."

Chapter Ten

Rosalie considered herself an excellent judge of people, and she had already decided Bess was one strange lady. But she kept coming back.

Sure, the money was good, Rosalie thought as she sat drinking a diet soda in Bess's basement office. And for a woman with a retirement plan, that had to be number one. Yet it was more than making an extra buck that kept her taking the trip up and across town several days each week. More, too, that kept her hanging around after they finished what Bess liked to call 'consulting sessions.'

Rosalie was human enough to get a charge out of being connected, however remotely, to the entertainment world. She couldn't deny that she'd been excited, awed and impressed when she watched a couple of tapings.

But there was another factor, a much more basic one. Rosalie enjoyed Bess's company.

Besides being a strange lady, Bess had class. Rosalie didn't figure a person had to possess class to recognize it in another. Class wasn't just a matter of pedigree—though she'd discovered Bess had one. It was more than having an old lady in the DAR, or an old man in *Who's Who*. It was hazier than that. Though Rosalie couldn't quite come up with the terms she wanted, she had recognized in Bess those rare and often nebulous qualities, grace and compassion.

She was procrastinating over taking the trip back downtown by dawdling over her drink. Bess didn't seem to mind if Rosalie hung around while she worked. In the few weeks since they'd hooked up, Rosalie had noted that Bess worked hard and long. Harder, in Rosalie's opinion, than she herself, or any of the other ladies in her profession. Certainly Bess's hours were longer.

It amused Rosalie to compare the two. In fact, she and Bess had gotten into a very interesting discussion on the similarities and differences between Bess's selling her mind and Rosalie her body.

What a kick that had been, Rosalie thought now, while Bess typed and mumbled. Philosophical discussions weren't the norm in Rosalie's world.

The simple term she had not quite grasped for their relationship was *friendship*. They had become friends.

"How late you gonna work?" Rosalie asked, and Bess glanced up absently from the computer screen.

"Oh...not much longer." Her eyes were still slightly unfocused when she blew her hair away from them. Brock was on the verge of seducing Jessica. "I just had this idea for a little twist on a scene for tomorrow." She smiled then. It was quick, and a little wicked. "Of course, several members of the cast are going to want to murder me when I toss this at them in the morning. But that's show biz."

Rosalie took a drag on her cigarette. "What time did you get in here this morning?"

"Today? About nine-thirty. I was..." She thought of Alex. "Running a little late."

Lips pursed, Rosalie looked at the fake designer watch on her wrist. "And it's after seven now." Her grin flashed. "Girlfriend, you'd only put in half that many hours in my line of work."

"Yeah, but I get to sit down." Bess rubbed at the dull ache in the back of her neck. She really was going to have to work on her posture. "Hungry?" she asked. "Want to order something in?"

With a little tug of regret, Rosalie stabbed out the cigarette. "No. I gotta get to work, too."

"You could take the night off." Casually Bess ran a finger lightly over the keyboard. "Maybe we could catch a movie."

Chuckling, Rosalie dug in her purse for a mirror to check her makeup. "You said you weren't going to try to reform me."

"I lied." Bess sat back in her chair while Rosalie painted her mouth bloodred. She'd tried very hard not to pontificate, not to pressure, not to preach. And thought she had succeeded. But she hadn't tried not to care. That would have been useless. "I really worry about you. Especially since the last murder."

The odd twisting in Rosalie's stomach had her shifting her eyes from her compact mirror to Bess. She couldn't remember if anyone had ever worried about her before. Certainly not in years. "Didn't I tell you I could take care of myself?"

"Yes, but—"

"No buts about it, honey." With a second dip into her purse, Rosalie pulled out a stiletto. One flick of the wrist, and the long, razor-sharp blade zipped out. "What I can't handle, this can."

Bess managed to close her mouth, but her eyes stayed riveted to the knife. In the overhead lights, it gleamed silver, bright as sudden death. She couldn't say it was elegant. But it was fascinating, deathly fascinating. "Can I?"

With a shrug of her shoulders, Rosalie passed the weapon to her. "Don't mess with the blade," she warned. "It's as sharp as it looks."

Bess took a good grip on the handle, twisting her wrist this way and that, like a fencer. She wondered if Jade/Josie might carry one. She was already imagining a scene where the tormented Jade found the knife—maybe with the blade smeared with blood—in one of her practical handbags. No, her briefcase. Better.

"Have you ever—"

"Not yet." Rosalie held out a hand to take it back. "But there's always a first time." She pressed the button, and the blade whisked away again. "So don't loose any sleep over me." After dropping the weapon back into her bag, she took out an atomizer and sprayed scent generously on her skin. The air bloomed with roses. "Couple more months, I'll have enough put away. I'm going to be spending the winter in the Florida sunshine while you slog through dirty snow." She rose, tugging her tight off-the-shoulder top provocatively down, so that the rise of her breasts swelled invitingly over it. "See you around."

"Wait." Bess scrambled through her own purse and came up with her mini recorder. "If it won't bother your ethics, I thought you might use this." At Rosalie's wry glance, Bess's cheeks heated. "I don't mean to record that part. Just the streets, conversations with the other women, maybe a couple of, ah . . . transactions."

"You're the boss." Taking the recorder, Rosalie slipped it away.

"Be careful," Bess added, though she knew Rosalie would laugh.

She did, sending a last cocky look over her bare shoulder. "Girlfriend, I'm always careful."

Still chuckling, Rosalie headed down the narrow corridor toward the freight elevator. She was already picturing the way Bess's eyes would pop out when she listened to the tape and discovered that her "consultant" had recorded *everything*. The prospect of pulling such a fine joke had her grinning as the doors slid open. Her amusement died a quick death when Alex walked off.

While they eyed each other with mutual suspicion, Alex pressed two fingers to the Door Open button. "How's the moonlighting going, Rosalie?"

"It passes the time."

When she started past him, he raised an arm to block the elevator opening. "What do you know about Crystal LaRue?"

"I know she's dead." Rosalie fisted a hand on her hip, cocked it. "Something else you want?"

Alex let her see that her snide invitation only amused him. "What do you know about her before she was dead?"

"Nothing." She would have given him the same answer if she'd been Crystal's most intimate friend, but as it was, she was telling the simple truth. "I never met her. Heard she was new, didn't have a man yet."

"Now, I heard that, too," Alex said conversationally. "And I heard that Bobby wanted to make her one of his wives."

"Maybe. Bobby likes to start them young."

Alex struggled with his disgust. She'd been seventeen, he thought. A runaway who hadn't know the rules and would never have a chance to learn them. "Did Bobby roust her, put on the pressure?"

"Can't say."

"Can't say? Or won't?"

Rosalie opened the hand on her hip and began to drum her fingers there. "Listen, I don't know what Bobby did. I've been keeping out of his way lately."

Saying nothing, Alex studied her face. The bruising had faded. "Seems to me Bess is paying you enough that you could stay out of his way altogether."

"That's my business."

"And hers," Alex said evenly. "I don't want him finding out about this sideline of yours and going after her." His eyes were cold and passionless. "Then I'd have to kill him."

"You think I'd turn Bobby on to her?" Arrogance was sidelined as fury snapped into Rosalie's voice. "I *owe* her."

"What?"

"Respect," she said, with an innate and graceful dignity that had Alex softening. "She had me eat at her table. She even said I could stay in her extra bedroom. Like a guest." Her lips thinned at Alex's expression. "Don't sweat it, honey. I didn't take her up on it. Sure, she's paying me, and maybe you don't think that's any different than me taking money from some slob off the street. But she treats me like somebody. Not some *thing,* some*body.*" Embarrassed by her own vehemence, she shrugged. "She doesn't have the sense not to."

"She's got sense, all right. Not all good." Alex's lips twitched, even as Rosalie's did. "Maybe she hasn't gone so wrong here. I just don't want her hurt."

"Neither do I." Rosalie tapped a scarlet nail on his chest. "You got a bad case, cop. Stars in your eyes." The little wisp of envy came and went, almost unnoticed. "Make sure you keep them in hers, or you'll answer to me."

His grin flashed before he could prevent it. The charm of it nearly had Rosalie changing her mind about cops. "Yes, ma'am." Like Bess, he wanted to say something that would stop her from going back on the streets. Unlike Bess, he accepted that there was nothing that would do it.

"Maybe I see why she's so stuck on you." When he moved his blocking arm, she stepped into the elevator, turned. "You be good to her, Stanislaski. She deserves good."

The elevator doors clunked shut. Alex stood studying them a moment before he turned and wandered down the corridor to find Bess.

She was bent over the keys, rapping out a machine-gun fire of words onto the monitor. Her fingers moved like lightning, but her eyes were far away. In Mill-brook, he thought, smiling to himself.

She had her legs crossed under her, up on the chair. The way her shoulders were hunched, he imagined her muscles would complain loudly the moment she came back to earth.

She was wearing a skirt again, a little leather num-ber in bold blue that was hiked high up on her thighs. The hot-pink blouse she'd tucked into it should have clashed with her hair, but it didn't. The blouse looked like silk and was carelessly shoved up to her elbows. A half-dozen gold bracelets clanged at her wrist as she worked. Rings flashed on her fingers, and the big Gypsy hoops she wore at her ears peeked out of her tousled hair.

His heart ached with love for her. And his loins... Alex let out a little breath. He wanted, quite simply, to devour her. Inch by delicious inch.

What the hell was he going to do, he wondered, when she tried to slither out of his life? He was sure she would, as she'd done with others before. He could lock her up, carry her off. He could beg or threaten. He already knew he would do whatever he had to in order to keep her in his life.

What had ever made him think he would one day find some nice, pretty woman with simple tastes and a quiet style? Someone who would be content to sit home while he worked his crazy hours? Who would have and help him raise the houseful of children he so badly wanted?

With Bess, nothing was simple, nothing was quiet. She would never be content to sit home but would badger him incessantly, picking at him until he gave in and talked about the darker aspects of his work, those pieces of his life that he wanted to keep locked away from everyone who mattered. As for children . . . He didn't know how the devil to get and keep a ring on her finger, much less ask her to help make a family.

Being in love with her left him helpless, made him stupid, brought him a kind of fear he'd never faced as a cop. Not fear for his life. Fear for his heart.

He could only take his own advice and leave things as they were. Handle each day until she was so used to him she'd want to stay.

As he watched, she stopped typing, lifted a hand to her neck for a quick, impatient rub. Her skirt hiked higher as she shifted. It took all his control not to lick his lips. She punched a few buttons, had the machine clicking. A moment later, the printer beside her began to hum.

With a smile on his face and lust in his heart, Alex closed the door quietly at his back. Locked it.

She jumped like a rabbit when his hands came down on her shoulders. "Didn't anyone ever teach you to sit in a chair?"

"Alexi." She pressed a hand to her galloping heart. "You scared— Oh . . ." Her sigh was long and heart-felt as he massaged away the aches. "That's wonderful."

"You're going to do permanent damage if you keep sitting like that all day."

"I was planning on soaking in a hot tub for two or three days." She leaned into his hands.

"Where's Lori?"

"She wasn't feeling too terrific." As the printer continued to rattle, Bess closed her eyes. "I told her I was leaving, too. Then I snuck back. I wanted to make a few changes for tomorrow." She brought her hand up to one of his, skimming her fingers over it to the wrist. "You said you might have to work late."

"Lead fizzled. We'll work on tracing the heart necklace down, but that's better during business hours."

"Trace it down?"

"Hit the jewelers," he explained, "see if we can track down to when it was bought. Long shot, but..."

"Do you think the heart has a personal meaning for him?"

"Like some woman broke his heart, so he gives them a symbol of it before he whacks them?" He gave a little grunt as he continued to knead her muscles. "It's a little too obvious to dismiss. Psychiatric profile figures him as sexually inadequate on a normal level, so he pays for women to perform. He wants them and detests himself for that, as much as he detests them for being available. The fact that he goes through a short courtship routine shows that—" He broke off as she reached for a pad. "Hold on, McNee." He gave her shoulders a hard squeeze. "I don't know how you do it. One minute I'm thinking about getting you out of these clothes and the next you've got me talking about a case." He pressed a kiss to the top of her head. "No notes."

Her fingers retreated from the pad, but with obvious reluctance. "I like hearing you talk about your work. I want you to be able to talk to me about anything."

"Apparently I can. Even the stuff I don't want you to hear. I've got a problem with you, Bess. You won't let me tuck you into that nice safe corner where I want you to be."

"You only think that's where you want me to be." Smiling, she tugged his hand around so that she could kiss it. "You like me right where I am." Turning his hand over, she pressed her lips to his palm. "I'm going to stay there."

She felt his fingers tense, then relax slowly as he spread them over her cheek. "I was watching you while you worked."

A rippling thrill raced through her at the words and at the shimmer of desire she heard in them. "Were you?"

"And thinking." His hands slid down over her breasts, sampled their weight, molded them. "Fantasizing."

Her head fell back against the chair. Her breathing quickened. "About?"

"The things I'd like to do with you." Through layers of silk, he caught her nipples, tugging gently. "To you."

When she tried to shift in the chair to face him, he increased the pressure, held her still. Her dazzled eyes focused on the monitor. She could still see the ghost of herself there, and his hands moving. Sliding. Stroking.

Impossibly erotic to see, and to feel. Dry-mouthed, she watched his fingers undo her buttons and saw the dark shadow of his hair as he pressed a hot mouth to her throat. She lifted a hand, hooked it around his neck as she tilted her head to offer more.

"I can shut down in thirty seconds."

He bit her lightly, just above the collarbone. "I'm not going to give you a chance to shut down."

She laughed shakily, even as she lifted her other arm to capture him in a reverse embrace. "I meant the computer."

He would have laughed himself, but he'd stopped breathing. "I know what you meant."

"But I—" He slipped a hand under her skirt, and it was so sudden, so searing. Before she could gasp out in shock, he had driven her ruthlessly to the peak.

"I watched you." Each word burned his throat as she poured into his hand. "I wanted you." Half demented, he whipped her up again, pressing his face into her neck as her body shuddered, shuddered. "Do you remember the first time I found you here?"

"What?" She couldn't remember her own name. There was only this need he was ruthlessly building inside her again. "Alexi, please. Come home with me. I need—" This time she cried out as the third high, hard wave swamped her.

"I wanted you then." In one violent move, he spun her chair around and dragged her to her feet, and her already weakened system went limp at what she read in his face. "Let me show you exactly what I wanted."

This wasn't the smooth and patient lover of the night before. This man with the fierce eyes and bruising hands wouldn't cuddle her and whisper exotic endearments. This was the warrior she'd only glimpsed. He would plunder. Whether or not she was ready, he was showing her that dark, reckless side of him that he kept so tightly controlled.

In the moment when he stared at her, the look in his eyes hot and concentrated, she understood that excitement took a twist into the primitive when it carried a touch of fear.

He fisted a hand in her hair and yanked her against him. His body was like rock, vibrating from deep within, as if from an erupting volcano. For that moment, there was only the strength and the fury of the inevitable.

His mouth burned over hers, his tongue diving deep, while his free hand tugged the snap of her skirt free. He wanted her flesh, craved it. That heated silk, those alluring curves and taut muscles. Time and place had lost all impact. There was only here. Only now. Only her.

Shivery fingers of fear ran up her spine. She hadn't known what it was to be wanted this way. It was so huge, so violent, so glorious. Before, he had given her more than she had ever dreamed of. Now, he seemed compelled to give her more than she had ever *dared* dream.

Beside them, the printer stopped its practical clatter and dropped into a hum. The low, waiting sound was drowned out by the thundering of her heart. The bright working lights overhead seemed to dim as he took her hips and pressed her hard against him.

"You make a war inside me," he muttered as his teeth scraped roughly down her throat. "There's no end to it. No peace from it. Say my name. I want to hear you say my name."

"Alexi." When his lips crushed down on hers again, he felt her breathe it, warm, into his mouth. "Take me. Now."

The wild need slammed into her so that her mouth was as turbulent, her hands as frantic. Dozens of tiny explosions burst inside her body, merging into one huge tumult of sensation that battered, bruised and bewitched. She was all but sobbing with it as she tugged and pulled at his clothes.

She was quivering for him. Couldn't stop. The power and pressure growing inside her was all but unbearable. And the heat, the furnace blast of heat, had her skin slicked and her head spinning. Glorying in it, she brought her mouth to his bare shoulder, savoring the taste of flesh. His busy, bruising hands had her bearing down with teeth and nails. His breath hissed in her ear as she reached down to curl impatient fingers around him.

Confused and tangled phrases whirled in his mind. He heard them burst from his lips to hang on the thick air as he fought to catch his breath. On an oath, he gripped her shoulders and hauled her back.

Her face was flushed, her eyes were glowing. He'd marked that ivory skin. He could see where his fingers had pressed, where his roughened cheeks had scraped. But the part of him that would have been shocked by his lack of care was far overshadowed by a dark and desperate desire to conquer, to consume. To mate.

He saw them now as brands, signs that made her his. Only his.

With a jerk of his head, he tossed his hair back. The way it swayed and settled had new emotion burning her throat. Naked, muscles bunched as if to fight, he looked so magnificent he dazzled her eyes.

Then he looked at her, and the smile that had nearly formed on her face froze into wonder.

"No one makes you feel like this but me."

His accent had thickened, and the sound of it sent chills along her heated skin. She could only shake her head.

"No one touches you like me." He took his hands from her shoulders and gripped the bodice of her chemise. "No one has you, ever again, but me."

"Alexi—"

But he shook his head. He could feel her heart pounding under his hands, and his own chest was heaving. "Understand me. You're mine now." Her eyes widened with shock as he jerked his hands and ripped the chemise in half. "All of you."

He pushed her back against the table, watching the play of stunned excitement over her face. Yes, he wanted to excite her. And shock her. Stagger her.

His fingers dug into her hips as he lifted her. He was braced, straining like a stallion at the bit. "Hold on to me," he demanded, but her fluttering hands slid off his sweat-slick arms. His breath heaved out, his fingers dug into her smooth, taut flesh. "Hold!"

She met his eyes then, and felt that wild whip of power. Drunk on it, she gripped his hair and wrapped her legs around him. When he plunged inside her, her body arched back, absorbing that first rocketing flash of heat. It was like being consumed from the inside out.

She felt the cool surface of the table against her back first, then his weight on her. Greedy for more, she tightened around him, matching his fast, frantic rhythm, dragging his mouth back to hers so that they could echo the intimacy with their tongues.

He lost himself. There was only her now, and the need to possess her. The desperate craving to be possessed by her. Images reeled through his brain, all dark and sharp-edged, until he thought he would go mad.

And went mad.

In a frenzy of movement, he dragged her farther onto the table, crushing papers, knocking aside empty cups, scattering pencils. He couldn't take his eyes from her face, the way her eyes clouded, like fog over moss, the way her lips trembled with each gasping breath. There was a bloom on her skin now, a rose under glass. He was hammering himself into her, empowered by a rabid fury of emotion that had its razor-tipped fingers around his throat.

Too much, she thought frantically. Never enough. The harsh overhead lights fractured into rainbows that blinded her eyes. They seemed to arch around his head, but she didn't think of angels. His eyes were so dark, so fiercely focused. Even as her own grew leaden, she refused to close them.

Oh, to watch him wanting her. Taking her.

She couldn't understand the words he murmured, over and over again. But she understood what was in those eyes. They were tearing each other apart, and they couldn't stop. The animal had taken over, and it had diamond-sharp claws and jagged teeth.

There was nothing left but the sound of their mixed labored breathing, the solid slap of flesh against flesh, and the heady scent of hot, desperate sex.

She felt his body go rigid, felt the rippling muscles in the arms she gripped turn to stone. He groaned out her name as his eyes sharpened like daggers. When he poured himself into her, she cried out in triumph, then again in wonder as he drove her over that crumbling edge with him.

The strength that had screamed through him switched off like a light, and he collapsed, panting, his full weight on her. Fighting for breath, he wallowed in her hair, drawing in the scent of it and the fragrance they'd made together. He couldn't find his center, the focus that was so vital for survival. He no longer had one without her.

God, he could feel her vibrating beneath him, shuddering from the aftershocks. And there were tears mixed with the dew of sweat on her face.

With breath still burning his lungs, he levered himself on his elbows and shook his head to try to clear it. At the movement, she made a small, whimpering sound in her throat that both aroused and dismayed. Trying to find the gentleness that had always been so easy for him, he shifted their positions and began to stroke her hair, her shoulders, her back.

Murmuring apologies, he cradled her like a child. "*Milaya,* I'm sorry. I hurt you. I must have hurt you. Don't cry."

"I'm not crying." But, of course, she was. He could feel the tears fall even as she ran kisses over his face and throat. "Just tell me you love me. Please tell me you love me."

"I love you. Shh." He covered her mouth tenderly with his. "You know I love you."

"I love you." She pressed those wet, shaky kisses to his cheeks, to his jaw. "You have to believe that I love you."

A hot fist clenched in his gut, but he kept his hands gentle. "Just let me hold you."

Tearing up again, she pressed her face to his shoulder. "Even now you don't believe me. Alexi, what more can I do?"

"I believe you." But they both knew he said it only to comfort. "You belong to me. I believe that."

"You're everything I want." She relaxed against him, satisfied that he would take that much.

"No more tears?"

"No."

He tilted her chin up to search her face. "How badly did I hurt you?"

"I don't think the results will be in for days." She smiled a little. "How badly did I hurt you?"

His eyes narrowed, and her smile widened. "You're not . . . upset?"

"About what?"

"I was an animal." With a hand that had yet to steady, he brushed her tumbled hair out of her face. "I took you on a table like a lunatic."

"I know." After one long, satisfied sigh, she slid her body lazily over his. "It was wonderful."

"Yes?" Guilt began to turn to pride. "You liked it?"

After being so thoroughly ravished, it wasn't difficult to stroke his ego. "It was like being dragged off by some barbarian. I couldn't even understand what you were saying. It was exciting." She kissed his cheek. "Frightening." And the other. "It was also the most erotic experience of my life."

"You were crying."

"Alexi." She touched a hand to his face. "You didn't just overpower me. You overwhelmed me. No one's ever made me feel more wanted. More irresistible."

"I can't resist you, but I'm sorry I put bruises on you."

"I don't mind—under the circumstances." After another luxurious sigh, she glanced around the room. "I don't know how I'll ever work in here again, though."

Now he grinned, wickedly. "Maybe it'll inspire you."

"There is that." She shifted to straddle him and watched his sleepy eyes skim down to her breasts and back. Possibilities, she thought. There were definite possibilities in that look. "Being a cop, I imagine you've been through arduous physical training."

The possibilities had occurred to him, as well. "Absolutely."

"And you'd probably have amazing recuperative powers."

His brow lifted. "Under the right conditions."

"Good." To be certain she created them, she ran her hands over his still-gleaming chest.

With a half laugh, he caught her wrists. "McNee, wouldn't you rather pick this up in bed?"

For an answer, she leaned over, letting her lips hover a breath away from his. The tip of her tongue darted out to trace the shape of his mouth, to dip teasingly inside, then retreat. Slowly, she tilted her head. Softly, she tasted his lips. Achingly, achingly, she deepened the kiss.

"Does that give you a clue, Detective?"

Chapter Eleven

"I can't believe you want to spend the best part of a Saturday morning in a sweaty gym." Alex was stalling, even as he walked with Bess up the iron steps that led to Rocky's.

"It's your sweaty gym," Bess said, and kissed him.

The past few days had been almost like a honeymoon, she thought. If she took out the hours they'd both been at work. But they'd made the most of what time they'd had together, snuggling on the couch in her place, cooking a meal in his, wrestling in bed in both.

She was starting to hope that he believed she loved him. And, once he did, she wanted nothing more than for them to take that next step. The step that would lead to an authentic honeymoon, with all the trimmings.

"You picked me up at my gym yesterday," she pointed out.

"That wasn't a gym." There was the faintest trace of a masculine sneer in his voice. "That was an exercise palace. Fancy lighting, piped-in music. All those mirrors."

"At least I'll be able to see when my butt starts to drop."

He gave it a friendly pat. "I'll let you know."

"Do, and die," she said smartly, and pushed through the frosted glass doors.

She immediately thought of every bad boxing film she'd ever seen. The huge room echoed with grunts and slaps and thumps. It smelled of mildew and sweat and... She took a testing sniff and decided she didn't want to know what else. There were exposed pipes along the ceilings and walls, and there was a hardwood floor that looked as though it had been gouged by spikes. The boxing ring that was set up in one corner was already occupied by two compact, dancing men in tiny shorts who were trying to pop each other in the eye.

A trio of punching bags hung at strategic points. A half-naked man with a body like a cement truck was currently trying to whip the tar out of one of them.

Weights were being employed as well. She watched tendons bulge and muscles bunch.

They didn't worry about mirrors and lighting here. Nor did she spot any of the high-tech equipment she was accustomed to. This was down-and-dirty—squat, sweat and punch. She sincerely doubted there would be a juice bar in the vicinity, either.

"Had enough?" Alex asked. He was obviously amused at the thought of her stripping down to her leotard and having a go with the boys.

Bess closed her mouth, then answered his grin with a cool stare. "I haven't even started yet."

It was his turn to drop his jaw when she peeled off her sweatshirt. Beneath she wore a snug, low-cut crop top in zigzagging stripes of green and purple. As she shimmied out of her baggy street shorts, he shoved the discarded shirt in front of her.

"Come on, Bess, put your clothes on. Sweet Lord." The bottom half was worse. Over formfitting tights she had on a teeny strip of spandex that covered little more than a G-string. "You can't wear that in here."

"Is it illegal?" She bent over to stuff her sweats into her gym bag and heard the heavy thump of weights as they were dropped. Maintaining position, she turned her head and smiled at the pop-eyed man staring at her.

The catcalls and whistles started immediately, the sound swelling and bouncing off the cinder-block walls. Alex was very much afraid there would be a riot—one he was likely to incite himself. "Damn it, put something on before I have to kill somebody."

"They look harmless." She straightened again and lifted her arms to tie the short curls at the nape of her neck into a stubby ponytail. "Anyway, I came to work out." With a challenging grin, she flexed a muscle. "How much can you bench-press?"

"McNee, don't you dare—" He broke off with an oath as she blithely strolled across the room to chat with the weight lifter. The two hundred pounds of muscle began to babble like a teenager. Alex had no choice but to send out a warning snarl, much as a guard dog might to a pack of encroaching wolves, before he went after her.

She pulled it off, of course. He should have known she would. The men started out drooling, kicked over into laughing and finally wound up competing with each other to show her the proper way to perform squat lifts, chin-ups and leg curls.

Before an hour was over, she'd been shown pictures of wives and children, listened to sob stories over sweethearts and stopped being ogled—unless it was at a discreet distance.

"You sure you want to do this?" Alex asked again, tapping his gloved hands together.

"Absolutely." She smiled at Rocky as he himself laced up her gloves. "I couldn't leave without one sparring match."

"You watch out for his left—it's a good one," Rocky advised her. "Kid could've been a contender if he hadn't wanted to be a cop."

She winked at Rocky. "I've got fast feet. He won't lay a glove on me."

Two of her new admirers held open the ropes for her so that she could step into the ring. Enjoying the sensation, she adjusted her padded helmet. "Aren't we supposed to wear those funny retainers?"

"The what— Oh, mouth guards?" He couldn't resist, and he leaned over and kissed her to an accompaniment of hoots. "Baby, I'm not going to hit you." In a friendly gesture, he tapped his gloves to hers. "Okay, put your hands up." When she did, lifting them toward the ceiling, he rolled his eyes. "It's not an arrest, McNee." Patiently he adjusted her hands until they were in a defensive position.

"Now, you want to guard, see? Keep your left up, keep it up. If I come in like this—" he did a slow-motion jab at her jaw "—you block, jab back. That's it."

"And I fake with my left," she said, and did so.

"If you want." Lord, she was sweet. "Now try for here." He tapped his own chin. "Go ahead, you don't have to pull it." When she punched halfheartedly, he shook his head. "No, you punch like a girl. Put your body behind it. Pretend I'm Dawn Gallagher."

Her eyes lit, and she swung full-out, only to come up solidly against his block. "Hey, that's good." Impressed, she swung again. "But I've got to move around, right? Fake you out with my grace and fancy footwork."

She did a quick boogie that had the onlookers clapping and Alex grinning at her. "You got style. Let's work on it."

He was enjoying himself, showing her the moves. And it certainly didn't hurt for a woman living in the city to learn how to defend herself with something more than an ammonia-filled water pistol.

"It's fun." She ducked her head as he'd shown her and tried two quick jabs with her left.

"Always room for another flyweight," Rocky called out to her. "Come on, Bess, body blow."

Chuckling, she aimed for Alex's midsection and dodged his light tap toward her chin. "You look so cute in gym shorts," she murmured.

"Don't try to distract me."

"Well, you do." She danced around him again, and, laughing, he turned toward her.

"Okay, that ought to—" He ended on a grunt when she connected hard with his jaw and set him down on his butt.

"Oh, God." She crouched instantly, battering his face with her gloves as she tried to stroke it. "Oh, Alexi, I'm sorry. Did I hurt you?"

He wiggled his jaw, sending her a dark look. "Right cross," he muttered as men climbed through the ropes to cheer and hold Bess's arms in the air.

"I'm really sorry," Bess said again as they started down the iron steps. But she was fingering the little bit of tarnished metal Rocky had pinned—with some ceremony—to her sweatshirt. "You said not to pull my punches."

"I know what I said." He'd be lucky if he didn't have a bruise, Alex thought. And how the hell would he explain that? "You only got through because I was finished."

She ran her tongue over her teeth and stepped outside. "Uh-huh."

"Don't get smart with me, McNee." He snatched her up and swung her around. "Or I'll demand a rematch."

Wildly in love, she tossed her arms around his neck. "Anytime."

"Oh, yeah? How about..." He trailed off with a grimace as his beeper sounded. "Sorry."

"It's all right." She only sighed a little as he tracked down a phone and called in. As she stood beside him, watching his face, listening to his terse comments, she realized that their plans for a picnic in the park and some casual shopping were about to go bust.

"You have your cop's face on," she said when he hung up. "Do you have to go in?"

"Yeah." But he didn't tell her they'd found another victim. It was bad enough that he was spoiling their plans for the day. "It's probably going to take a while. I'm really sorry, Bess."

"Look." She framed his face with her hands. "I understand. This is part of it."

He brought those hands to his lips. "I . . ." But he didn't tell her he loved her, because she would echo the words, and it made him nervous to hear them. "I appreciate it," he said instead. "And I'll make it up to you."

"Tell you what—why don't I finish up what I have to do, then stop by the market? I'll make dinner. Something that won't spoil if it has to be warmed up a couple of times."

Though his mind was already drifting away from her, he managed a pained smile. "You're going to cook."

"I'm not that bad. I'm not," she insisted with a bit of a huff when he grinned. "I only burned the potatoes the other night because you kept distracting me."

"I guess it's the least I can do." He kissed her lightly once, then again, longer. "I'll try to call."

"If you can." She waved him off, then stood watching while he jogged down into the subway. With a quick laugh, she spun around, hugging herself.

She felt just like a cop's wife.

"I hope you don't mind me dropping by."

"Of course not." Rachel took a look at the bulging shopping bags in Bess's hands. "Been busy?"

"Whenever I get started with that little plastic card, I can't seem to stop." She dumped her purchases inside the apartment door. "You look wonderful. How can you look wonderful less than a week after going through childbirth?"

"Strong genes." Pleased in general, and with Bess in particular, Rachel kissed her on both cheeks. "Come sit down."

"Thanks. I— Oops." She dipped into the bag and pulled out a gold foiled candy box. "For Mom."

"Oh." Rachel's eyes took on the glow a woman's get when she looks at a lover—or a five-pound box of exclusive chocolates. "I think you just became my best friend."

Chuckling, Bess dug into the bags again. "Well, I know that people tend to drop by with baby gifts." She held out a box wrapped in snowy white with bright red lollipops scattered over it. "And, though I couldn't resist the tradition, I figured you deserved something really sinful for yourself."

"I do." Rachel tucked the baby box under her other arm. "It's really sweet of you, Bess, and unnecessary. You and Alex already brought Brenna that wonderful stuffed dragon."

"That was from us. This is from me. It's a girl thing. I saw this tiny little white organdy dress with all these flounces and little pink bows and I couldn't resist."

Rachel's new-mother's heart melted. "Really?"

"I figure in another year she might want to wear motorcycle boots, so this may be your only chance to play dress-up."

"I swore that whatever I had, I wouldn't make sex-ist decisions in dress or attitude." She sighed over the box. "White organdy?"

"Six flounces. I counted."

"I can't wait to put her in it."

"Ah, company." Mikhail strode out of the bed-room with Brenna tucked in his arm. "Hello, Aunt Bess." He kissed both of her cheeks, then her mouth.

"You said you wouldn't wake her up." This from Rachel, who was already leaning over to coo.

"I didn't. Exactly. What's this?" Recognizing the gold foil box, he flipped it open and dived in.

"Mine," Rachel said in a huff. "If you eat more than one, I'll break your fingers."

"She was always greedy," he said over the first piece. "Where's Alexi?"

"He got called in."

"Good. Now you have time to sit down. I'll sketch you."

"Now?" Womanlike, Bess lifted a hand to her hair. "I'm not exactly dressed for it."

"I want your face." Obviously well used to making himself at home, he opened the drawer on an end ta-ble and rummaged for a pad. "Perhaps I'll do your body later. It's a good one."

Her laugh was quick. "Thanks."

"You might as well cooperate," Rachel told her, and crossed over to take the baby. "Once the artist in him takes over, you haven't got a chance."

"I'm flattered, really."

"There's no reason to be," he said absently as he unearthed a suitable pencil. "You have the face you were born with."

"Thank God that's not always true."

That caught his interest. "You had it fixed?"

"No. I just sort of grew into it."

"Not there," he told her before Bess could sit. "Over there, closer to the window in the light. Rachel, when do I get the drink you promised me?"

"On its way." She stopped nuzzling Brenna long enough to look up. "What can I get you, Bess?"

"Anything cold—and a shot at holding the baby."

"I can accommodate you on both counts." Rachel laid her daughter gently in Bess's arms. "She hardly ever cries. And I think her eyes may stay blue. Like Zack's."

"She's a beauty." Bess leaned down to brush her lips over the curling dark hair and to draw in the indescribably sweet scent of baby. "Like all of you."

"Move," Mikhail ordered his sister. "You're in my way."

Shooting off a mild Ukrainian insult, she headed for the kitchen.

"Talk if you like." Mikhail gestured with his pencil, and began to sketch.

"It's one of my best things." She'd already forgotten to be self-conscious. "Where's Sydney and Griff?"

"Griff has the sniffles." The pencil was moving with quick, deft strokes over the pad. "Sydney fusses over him, but she says *I'm* fussing over him and sends me out on errands."

"Which he does by coming by and plaguing me," Rachel called out.

"She's happy to see me," Mikhail said. "Because she's lonely, with Zack and Nick over checking on the progress of the new apartment."

"Oh, that's right, you're moving." Comfortable, Bess tucked up her legs. "Alexi mentioned it."

"We need a bigger place. Of course, it was supposed to be ready a month ago, but things never run on time. I'll miss this one," she said, coming back in with a tray of cold drinks. "And having Nick underfoot. But I imagine he'll like having this place to himself."

Bess reached for her drink with her free hand, gently jiggling the baby with the other. "I guess he had as big a crush on you as Freddie has on him."

For a moment, Rachel only stared. Then she let out her breath in a quiet laugh. "Alex said you saw things."

"Just part of the job."

Rachel didn't consider herself a slouch in the reading-people department. "So, how big a crush do you have on Alexi?"

"The biggest." Bess smiled and rubbed her cheek over Brenna's. "He thinks I'm flighty. Fickle. But I'm not. Not with him."

"Why would he think that?"

"I have a varied track record. But it's different with him." When Bess lowered her head to murmur to the baby, Rachel glanced at her brother. They exchanged a great deal without uttering a word. "It makes me envy people like your sister, Natasha," Bess went on. "Those three beautiful children, a husband who after years together still looks at her as if he can't believe she belongs to him. Work she loves. I envy all that."

"You'd like a family?"

"I never had one."

Rachel knew it was the lawyer in her, but she couldn't help moving along the line of questioning. "Does it bother you that he's a cop?"

"Bother me?" Bess's brows lifted in surprise. "No. Do you mean, will I worry? I suppose I will. But it's not something I could change, or that I want to change. I love who he is."

"He's making you sad," Mikhail said quietly.

"No." Bess's denial was quick enough to startle the dozing baby. She soothed her automatically as she shook her head. "No, of course he isn't."

"I see what's in your eyes."

He would, she realized, and felt the warmth creep into her cheeks. "It's only that I know he doesn't trust me—my feelings. Or, I suppose, the endurance of my feelings. It's not his fault."

"He was always one to pick things apart." There was brotherly disgust in Mikhail's voice. "Never one to take anything on faith. I'll speak to him."

"Oh, no." This time, she laughed. "He'd be furious with both of us. All that Slavic pride and male ego."

Instantly Mikhail's eyes narrowed. "What's wrong with that?"

"Nothing." She grinned at Rachel. "Not a thing. I'll just wear him down in my own way. In fact, I'm going to start tonight. I'm cooking dinner. I thought maybe I could call your mother, find out if he has a favorite dish."

"I can tell you that," Rachel offered. "Anything."

"Well, that certainly widens my choices. Do you think she'd mind if I called her, asked for some pointers? My kitchen skills are moderate at best."

"She'd love it." Rachel smiled to herself, knowing her mother would hang up the phone and immediately start planning the wedding.

* * *

It was after midnight when Alex let himself into Bess's apartment with the key she'd given him. He was punchy with fatigue, and his head was buzzing from too much coffee. Those were usual things, as much a part of his work as filing reports or following a lead. But the sick weight in his stomach was something new.

He would have to tell her.

She'd left the television on. In an old black-and-white movie a woman screamed in abject terror and fled down a moonlit beach. As he shrugged out of his jacket, Alex moved across the room to switch it off. Before he reached the set, he saw her, curled on the couch.

She'd waited for him. The sweetness of that speared through him as he crouched beside her. For so many years now, he'd come home alone, to no one. Gently he brushed the dark red curls from her cheek and replaced them with his lips. She stirred, murmuring. Her eyes fluttered open.

"I'm just going to carry you into bed," he whispered. "Go back to sleep."

"Alexi." She lifted a hand to rub over the cheek he hadn't shaved that morning. Her voice was thick with sleep, her eyes glazed with it. "What time is it?"

"It's late. You should have gone to bed."

She made a vague sound of disagreement and pushed up on one elbow. "I was waiting up, but the movie was so bad." Her laugh was groggy, and she rubbed her eyes like a child. "It zapped me." She circled her shoulders before leaning forward to kiss him. "You had a long day, Detective."

"Yeah." And maybe, because she was half-asleep, he could put off the rest. "So have you. I'll cart you in."

"No, I'm okay." She sat up, yawning. "Did you eat something?"

"I caught a sandwich. I'm really sorry, I tried to call."

"And got the machine," she said with a rueful nod. "Because I'd forgotten the paprika and had to run back out to the market."

"You cooked?" The idea both touched him and accented his guilt.

"I amazed myself." It felt good to settle against him when he joined her on the couch and slipped an arm around her. Cozy, right, and wonderfully simple. "Your mother's recipe for chicken and dumplings—Hungarian-style."

"*Csirke paprikas?*" Normally it would have made his mouth water. "That's a lot of work."

"It was a culinary adventure—and the cleaning lady will probably quit on Monday, after one look at the kitchen." She laughed up at him, then scrubbed her knuckles over his cheek when she caught the look in his eyes. "Don't worry. It'll heat up just fine for tomorrow's lunch. Then again…" She snuggled closer. "If you're feeling really guilty, I'll take you up on that ride to the bedroom—and whatever else you can think of."

But instead of chuckling and scooping her up, he pushed away to pace to the television and snap it off. "We have to talk."

His tone had nerves skittering in her stomach, but she nodded. "All right."

He thought it might be best—for both of them—if they had some of the brandy she had offered him during an earlier crisis. Trying out the words in his head, he walked to the lacquered cabinet.

"It's bad," she murmured, and pressed her lips together, hard. Her first thought was that he had changed his mind about her. That he had finally taken that good look she'd been afraid of and realized his mistake.

"It's bad," he concurred, then brought the snifters to the couch. "Here. Drink a little."

"It's all right. I don't make scenes."

He tilted the brandy toward her lips himself. "Just a little, *milaya*."

She closed her eyes and did as he asked. He couldn't say that sweet word to her in that loving tone if he'd changed his mind. "Okay." A deep breath, and she opened her eyes again.

"There was another murder last night."

"Oh, Alexi." Instantly the image of Crystal La-Rue's mangled body flashed behind her eyes. "Oh, God." She caught his hand in hers and squeezed. "Last night?"

"The desk clerk found her this morning. They had an arrangement. She only used that room for work, and he was ticked that she hadn't checked out and slipped him his usual tip." He was taking it slow, deliberately, so that the general horror would pass before he hit her with the specifics. Again he tipped the brandy up to her lips. "She'd rented the room three times last night. He caught a glimpse of the third john when they went up, so we've had him looking over mug shots most of the day."

"You'll catch him."

"Oh, yeah. There's no doubt about it this time. He didn't find the guy in the books, but he gave the police artist a fair description. We'll be broadcasting it. This time we should have his blood type, too. DNA. Couple of other things."

"You'll have him soon."

"Not soon enough. Bess, the woman..." His fingers tightened on hers, but he told her the worst as gently as he knew how. "It was Rosalie."

She only stared, and he watched, helpless, as the color simply slid out of her face. "No." She was tugging her hand from his, but he only held tighter. "You're wrong. You made a mistake. I just saw her. I just talked to her a couple of days ago."

"There's no mistake." His voice toughened, for her sake. "I ID'd her myself. Rechecked that with prints, and the desk clerk's ID. Bess, it was Rosalie."

The moan came out brokenly as she wrapped her arms around herself and began to rock. "Don't," she said when he tried to gather her close. "Don't, don't, don't."

She sprang up, needing the distance, desperate to find something to do with the helpless rage that was building inside her. "She didn't have to die. It isn't right. It isn't right for her to die like that."

"It's never right."

It was his tone, the cool detachment of it, that had her whirling on him. "But she was just a hooker. Don't get involved, right? Don't feel anything. Isn't that what you told me?"

He went very still, as if she'd pulled a gun and taken aim. "I guess I did."

"I wanted to help her, but you told me I couldn't. You told me it was a waste of my time and energy. And you were right, weren't you, Alexi? How fine it must be to always be so right."

He took the blow. What else could he do? "Why don't you sit down, Bess? You'll make yourself sick."

She wanted to break something, to smash it—but nothing was precious enough. "I *cared,* damn you. I cared about her. She wasn't just a story line to me. She was a person. All she wanted was to go south, buy a trailer." When her breath began to hitch, she covered her mouth with her hands. "She shouldn't have died like that."

"I wish I could change it." The bitter sense of failure turned his voice to ice. "I wish to God I could." Before he realized the glass was leaving his hand, he was heaving the snifter against the wall. "How do you know what I felt when I walked into that filthy room and found her like that? How the hell do you know what it's like to face it and know you couldn't stop it? She was a person to me, too."

"I'm sorry." The tears that spilled over now spilled for all of them. "Alexi, I'm sorry."

"For what?" He tossed back. "It was the truth."

"Facts. Not truth." He'd tried to soften the blow, to cushion her when his own emotions were raw. He'd needed to comfort. His eyes had been dazed with fatigue and pain and the kind of grief she might never understand, but he'd needed to shield her. And she hadn't allowed it. "Hold me, please. I need you to hold me."

For a moment she was afraid he wouldn't move. Then he crossed to her. Though his arms were rigid with tension, they came around her.

"I didn't mean to hurt you," she murmured, but he only shook his head and stroked her hair. Grieving, she turned her face into his throat. "I wanted to make it a lie somehow. To make you wrong so it could all be wrong." She squeezed her eyes closed and held tight. "She was somebody."

He stared blankly over her shoulder as he remembered one of the last things Rosalie had said to him. *She treats me like somebody.* "I know."

"You'll catch him," she said fiercely.

"We'll catch him. We'll put him away. He won't hurt anybody else." Though her words still scraped against him, he rocked her. He would tell her the rest and hoped it helped. "She had a knife."

"I saw it. She showed me."

"She used it. I don't know how bad she hurt him, but she put up a hell of a fight. It's recorded."

"Recorded?" Eyes dull with shock, she leaned back. "My God. The tape. I gave her my mini recorder."

"I figured as much. For whatever consolation it is, the fact that you did give it to her, and she decided to use it, is going to make a difference. A big one."

"You heard them," she said through dry lips. "You heard—"

"We got everything, from the deal on the street until . . . the end. Don't ask me, Bess." He lifted a hand to cup her face. "Even if I could tell you what was on the tape, I wouldn't."

"I wasn't going to ask. I don't think I could bear to know what happened in that room."

Calmer now, he searched her face. "I've only got a few hours. I have to go in first thing in the morning. Do you want me to stay with you tonight, or would you rather I go?"

She'd hurt him more than she'd realized. Perhaps the only way she could heal the wound was to admit, and to show him, that she needed comfort. Needed it from him. Drawing him close, she laid her head on his shoulder.

"I want you with me, Alexi. Always. And tonight—I don't think I'd make it through tonight without you."

She began to cry then. Alex picked her up and carried her to the couch, where they could lie down and grieve together.

Chapter Twelve

Judd flexed his hand on the steering wheel as he turned on West Seventy-sixth. He wasn't nervous this time. He was eager. The idea of bringing Wilson J. Tremayne III—a U.S. senator's grandson—in for questioning in the murders of four women had him chafing at the bit.

They had him, Judd thought. He knew they had the creep. The artist's sketch, the blood type, the voice-print. It had been quick work on that, he mused. Flavored with luck. Bess's tape had been one of those twisted aspects of police work that never failed to fascinate him.

It was Trilwalter who'd identified Tremayne from the sketch. Judd remembered that the boss had taken a long, hard look at the artist's rendering and then ordered Alex to the newspaper morgue. The desk clerk had picked the reprint of Tremayne's newspaper picture from a choice of five.

From there, Alex had used a connection at one of the local television stations and had finessed a videotape of Tremayne campaigning for his grandfather. The lab boys had jumped right on it, and had matched the voice to the one on Bess's tape.

It still made him queasy to think about what had been on that tape, but that was something he didn't want to show to Alex. Just as he knew better than to let Alex spot his eagerness now.

"So," he said casually, "you think the Yankees have got a shot this year?"

Alex didn't even glance over. He could all but taste his partner's excitement. "When a cop starts licking his lips, he forgets things. Miranda rights, probable cause, makes all kinds of little procedural mistakes that help slime ooze out of courtrooms and back onto the street."

Judd clenched his jaw. "I'm not licking my lips."

"Malloy, you'll be drooling any minute." Alex looked over at the beautiful old building while Judd hunted up a parking space. The Gothic touches appealed to him, as did the tall, narrow windows and the scattering of terrace gardens. Tremayne lived on the top floor, in a plush two-level condo with a view of the park and a uniformed doorman downstairs.

He came and went as he pleased, wearing his Italian suits and his Swiss watch.

And four women were dead.

"Don't take it personally," Alex said when they got out of the car. "Stanislaski's rule number five."

But Judd was getting good, very good, at reading his partner. "You want him as bad as I do."

Alex looked over, his eyes meeting, then locking on Judd's. There wasn't eagerness in them or excitement or even satisfaction. They were all cold fury. "So let's go get the bastard."

They flashed their badges for the doorman, then rode partway up in the elevator with a plump middle-aged woman and her yipping schnauzer. Alex glanced up and spotted the security camera in the corner. It might come in handy, he thought. The DA would have to subpoena the tapes for the nights of the murders. If they were dated and timed, so much the better. But, if not, they would still show Tremayne going and coming.

The schnauzer got off at four. They continued on to eight. Side by side, they approached 8B.

Though the door was thick, Alex could hear the strains of an aria from *Aida* coming from the apartment. He'd never cared much for opera, but he'd liked this particular one. He wondered if it would be spoiled for him now. He rang the buzzer.

He had to ring it a second time before Tremayne answered. Alex recognized him. It was almost as though they were old friends now that Alex had pored over the newspaper shots and stories, the videotape. And, of course, he knew his voice. Knew it when it was calm, when it was amused and when it was darkly, sickly, thrilled.

Dressed in a thick velour robe that matched his china-blue eyes, Tremayne stood dripping, rubbing a thick monogrammed towel over his fair hair.

"Wilson J. Tremayne?"

"That's right." Tremayne glanced pleasantly from face to face. He didn't have the street sense to smell cop. "I'm afraid you've caught me at a bad time."

"Yes, sir." Never taking his eyes off Tremayne's, Alex took out his badge. "Detectives Stanislaski and Malloy."

"Detectives?" Tremayne's voice was bland, only mildly curious, but Alex saw the flicker. "Don't tell me my secretary forgot to pay my parking tickets again."

"You'll have to get dressed, Mr. Tremayne." Still watching, Alex replaced his shield. "We'd like you to come with us."

"With you?" Tremayne eased backward a step. Judd noted that his hand eased down toward the doorknob, closed over it. Knuckles whitened. "I'm afraid that would be very inconvenient. I have a dinner engagement."

"You'll want to cancel that," Alex said. "This may take a while."

"Detective—?"

"Stanislaski."

"Ah, Stanislaski. Do you know who I am?"

Because it suited him, because he wanted it, Alex let Tremayne see the knowledge. "I know exactly who you are, Jack." Alex allowed himself one quick flash of pleasure at the fear that leaped into Tremayne's eyes. "We're going downtown, Mr. Tremayne. Your presence is requested for questioning on the murders of four women. Mary Rodell." His voice grew quieter, more dangerous, on each name. "Angie Horowitz, Crystal LaRue and Rosalie Hood. You're free to call your attorney."

"This is absurd."

Alex slapped a hand on the door before Tremayne could slam it shut. "We can take you in as you are—

and give your neighbors a thrill. Or you can get dressed.''

Alex saw the quick panic and was braced even as Tremayne turned to run. He knew better—sure he did—but it felt so damn good to body-slam the man up against that silk-papered wall. A small, delicate statue tipped from its niche and bounced on the carpet. When he hauled Tremayne up by the lapels, he saw the gold chain, the dangling heart with a crack running through it that was the twin of the one they had in evidence. And he saw the fresh white bandage that neatly covered the wounds Rosalie had inflicted as she fought for her life.

"Give me a reason." Alex leaned in close. "I'd love it."

"I'll have your badges." Tears began to leak out of Tremayne's eyes as he slid to the floor. "My grandfather will have your badges."

In disgust, Alex stood over him. "Go find him some pants," he said to Judd. "I'll read him his rights."

With a nod, Judd started for the bedroom. "Don't take it personally, Stanislaski."

Alex glanced over with something that was almost a smile. "Kiss off, Malloy."

They had him cold, Alex thought as he turned into Bess's building. They could call out every fancy lawyer on the East Coast, and it wouldn't mean a damn thing. The physical evidence was overwhelming— particularly since they'd found the murder weapon in the nightstand drawer.

Opportunity was unlikely to be a problem, and as for motive—he'd leave that up to the shrinks. Undoubtedly they'd cop an insanity plea. Maybe they'd even pull it off. One way or the other, he was off the streets.

It went a long way toward easing the bitterness he'd felt over Rosalie's death. He hoped it helped Bess with her grief.

He'd nearly called her from the station, but he'd wanted to tell her face-to-face. As he waited for the elevator, he shifted the bunch of lilacs he held. Maybe it was a weird time to bring her flowers, but he thought she needed them.

Stepping into the car, he tucked a hand in his pocket and felt the jeweler's box. It was even a weirder time to propose marriage. But he knew he needed it.

It scared him just how much he'd come to depend on having her with him. To talk to him, to listen to him, to make him laugh. To make love with him. He knew he was rushing things, but he justified it by assuring himself that if he got her to marry him quickly enough, she wouldn't have time to change her mind.

She believed she was in love with him. After they were committed, emotionally and legally, he would take as much time as necessary to make certain it was true.

The elevator opened, and Alex dug for his keys. They'd order in tonight, he decided. Put on some music, light some candles. He grimaced as he fit the key into the lock. No, she'd probably had that routine before, and he'd be damned if he'd follow someone else's pattern. He'd have to think of something else.

He opened the door with his arms full of nodding lilacs, his mind racing to think of some clever, innovative way to ask Bess to be his wife. The color went out of his face and turned his eyes to midnight. He felt something slam into his chest. It was like being shot.

She was standing in the center of the room, her laughter just fading away. In another man's arms, her mouth just retreating from another man's lips.

"Charlie, I—" She heard the sound of the door and turned. The bright, beaming smile on her face froze, then faded away like the laughter. "Alexi."

"I guess I should have knocked." His voice was dead calm. Viciously calm.

"No, of course not." There were butterflies in her stomach, and their wings were razor-sharp. "Charlie, this is Alexi. I've told you about him."

"Sure. Think I met you at Bess's last party." Lanky, long-haired and obviously oblivious to the tension throbbing in the air, he gave Bess's shoulders a squeeze. "She gives the best."

Alex set the flowers aside. One fragile bloom fell from the table and was ignored. "So I've heard."

"Well, I've got to be going." Charlie bent to give Bess another kiss. Alex's hands clenched. "You won't let me down?"

"Of course not." She worked up a smile, grateful that Charlie was too preoccupied to sense the falseness of it. "You know how happy I am for you, Charlie. I'll be in touch."

He went out cheerfully, calling out a last farewell before he shut the door. In the silence, Alex noticed the music for the first time. Violins and flutes whispered out of her stereo. Very romantic, he thought, and his teeth clenched like his fists.

"Well." Her eyes were burning dry, though her heart was weeping. "I can see I should explain." She walked over to the wine she'd poured for Charlie and topped off her glass. "I can also see that you've already made up your mind, so explanations would be pointless."

"You move fast, Bess."

She was glad she had her back to him for a moment. Very glad, because her hand trembled as she lifted the wine. "Do you think so, Alexi?"

"Or maybe you've been seeing him all along."

"You can say that?" Now she turned, and the first flashes of anger burst through her. "You can stand there and say that to me?"

"What the hell do you expect me to say?" he shot back. He didn't go near her. Didn't dare. "I walk in here and find you with him. A little music, a nice bottle of wine." He wished he had been shot. It couldn't possibly hurt more than this bite of betrayal. "Do you think I'm an idiot?"

"No. No, I don't." She needed to sit, but she locked her knees straight. "But I must be to have been so careless as to have an assignation here when you were bound to find me out." Her eyes were like glass as she toasted him. "Caught me."

He took a step forward, stopped himself. "Are you going to tell me you didn't sleep with him?"

In the thrum of silence, the flutes sang. "No, I'm not going to tell you that. I'm not ashamed that I once cared enough for a very good man to be intimate with him. I'd tell you that I haven't been with Charlie or anyone else since I met you, but the evidence is against me, isn't it, Detective?"

She was so tired, Bess thought, so terribly tired, and the scent of the lilacs made her want to weep. Rosalie's funeral had been that morning, and she'd quietly made the arrangements herself. She'd gone alone, without mentioning it to Alex. But she'd needed him.

"You let him kiss you."

"Yes, I let him kiss me. I've let lots of men kiss me. Isn't that the problem?" She set down the wine before she could do something rash, like tossing it to the floor. "You didn't come to me a virgin, Alexi, nor did I expect you to. That's one of the big differences between us."

"There's a bigger difference between a virgin and a—"

He broke off, appalled with himself. He wouldn't have meant it. Stumbling, horrified apologies whirled through his head. But he could see by the way her head jerked up, the way her color drained, that there would be no taking back even the unsaid.

"I think," she said in an odd voice, "you'd better go."

"We haven't finished."

"I don't want you here. Even a whore can choose."

His face was as pale as hers. "Bess, I didn't mean that. I could never mean that. I want to understand—"

"No, you don't." She cut him off, her voice so thick with tears that she had to fight for every word. "You never wanted to understand, Alexi. You never wanted to hear the one thing I needed you to believe. Now the only thing you need to understand is that I don't want to see you again."

He felt something rip apart in his gut. "You can't have that."

"If you don't leave now, I'll call Security. I'll call your captain, I'll call the mayor." Desperation was rising like a flood. "Whatever it takes to keep you away from me."

His eyes narrowed, sharpened. "You can call God Almighty. It won't stop me."

"Maybe this will." She gripped her hands tightly together and looked just over his shoulder. "I don't love you, I don't want you, I don't need you. It was fun while it lasted, but the game's over. You can let yourself out."

She turned away and walked quickly up the stairs. There had been hurt in his eyes. If there had been anger, she knew, he would have come after her, but there had been hurt, and she made it to the bedroom alone. With her hands over her face, she waited, biting back sobs, until she heard the door close downstairs. With a sound of mourning, she lowered herself to the floor and tasted her own tears. They were bitter.

Impatient and unsympathetic, Mikhail paced the floor of Alex's sparsely furnished apartment. "You don't answer your phone," he was saying. "You don't return messages." He kicked a discarded shirt aside. The apartment was a shambles. "Lucky for you I came instead of Mama. She'd box your ears for living like a pig."

"I gave the staff the month off." With the concentrated care of the nearly drunk, Alex poured another glass of vodka from the half-empty bottle on the table.

"And drinking alone in the middle of the day."

"So, join me." Alex gestured carelessly toward the kitchen, where dishes were piled high. "Bound to be a clean glass somewhere."

Mikhail washed one out before coming back to the table. He sat, poured. "What is this, Alexi?"

"Celebration. My day off." Alex took a swallow and waited for the vodka to join the rest swimming through his system. "I caught the bad guy." With a half laugh, he toasted himself. "And lost the girl."

Mikhail drummed his fingers on the table as he drank. It was no less than he'd expected. "You fought with Bess?"

"Fought?" Lips pursed, Alex studied the clear, potent liquid in his glass. "I don't know that's the term, exactly. Found her with another man."

Mikhail's glass froze halfway to his lips. "You're wrong."

"Nope." Alex reached for the bottle with an almost steady hand. "Walked in and found her lip-locked to this guy she used to be engaged to. Bess has this hobby of getting engaged."

Mikhail merely shook his head. Something was not quite right with this picture. "Did you kill him?"

"Thought about it." Before he drank again, Alex ran his tongue over his teeth. Good, he thought. They were nearly numb. The rest would follow. "Too damn bad I'm a cop."

"What was her explanation?"

"Didn't give me one. Got pissed, is all." He set the glass down so that he could use both hands to rub his face.

"Because you accused without trusting."

"I didn't accuse," Alex shot back, then pressed his fingers to his burning eyes. "I didn't have to. What I didn't say was unforgivable. She tossed me out on my ear, but not before she told me she didn't love me anyway."

"She lies." Before Alex could lift his glass again, Mikhail grabbed his wrist. "I tell you, she lies. A few days ago she visited Rachel and the baby. I made her sit for me and sketched her while she talked of you. There's no mistaking what I saw in her eyes, Alexi. You're blind if you haven't seen it yourself."

He had seen it, and the pain of remembering what he'd seen clawed through him so that he stumbled to his feet as if to escape it. "She falls in love easily."

"So? There is love, and love. How many times have you taken the fall?"

"This is the first."

"For this kind, yes. There were others."

"They were different."

"Ah." Patient and amused, Mikhail held up a finger. "So it's okay for you to play with love until you find the truth, but it's not okay for Bess."

"It's—" Put that way, it was tough to argue with. Especially when his head was reeling. "Damn it, I was jealous. I have a right to be jealous."

"You have a right to make an ass of yourself, too." Pleased, now that he knew it could be fixed, Mikhail kicked back and crossed his booted feet. "Did you?"

"Big-time." Alex swayed, then sat down heavily. "I was going to ask her to marry me, Mik. I had the ring in my pocket and these stupid lilacs. I was scared to death she'd say yes. More scared that she'd say no." He propped his spinning head in his hands. "What the hell was she doing kissing that son of a bitch?"

"Maybe if you had asked nicely, she would have told you."

With a lopsided grin, Alex turned his bleary eyes on his brother. "Would you have asked nicely?"

"No, I would have broken his arms, maybe his legs, too. Then I would have asked." With a sigh, Mikhail patted Alex's shoulder. "But that is me. You were always more impulsive."

"We could go find him." Alex considered and, warming to the idea, leaned over to give Mikhail a sloppy hug. "We'll go beat him up together. Like old times."

"We'll try something different." Rising, Mikhail hauled Alex to his feet.

"Where we going?"

"I'm going to put you in a cold shower until your head's clear."

Alex staggered and linked an arm around his brother's neck. "What for?"

"So you can go find your woman and grovel."

Unsure of his footing, Alex stared at the tilting floor. "I don't wanna grovel."

"Yes, you do. It's best to get used to it before you marry her. I have more experience in this."

"Oh, yeah?" Enjoying the idea of his big brother crawling at Sydney's feet, he grinned as Mikhail thrust him, fully clothed, into the shower. "Can I watch next time?"

"No." With immense satisfaction, Mikhail turned the cold water on full and listened to his brother's pained shout bounce viciously on the tiles. "This is a very good start," he decided.

"You son of a bitch." They were both laughing when Alex grabbed Mikhail in a headlock and dragged him under the spray.

* * *

He was nearly sober by the time he walked into Bess's office, but he wasn't laughing. It was hard to laugh when your throat was thick with nerves.

He was going to be reasonable, he promised himself. They would discuss the entire matter like civilized adults. And if she didn't give him the right answers, he'd strangle her. He could always arrest himself afterward.

But he only saw Lori sitting at the keyboard, frantically typing. "I'll have the damn changes by six," she called out. Her brow was furrowed in concentration as she glanced up. Her eyes frosted over.

"What the hell do you want?"

"I need to see Bess."

"You're out of luck." Nobody hurt her friend and got away with it. Nobody. "She's not here."

"Where?"

She offered an anatomically impossible suggestion, offered it so coolly he nearly smiled. But it wasn't enough. She leapt up and slammed the door shut. Locked it. "Sit down, buster, I've got an earful for you."

"Tell me where she is."

"When hell freezes over. Do you know what you did to her?" She took the flat of her hand to push him back. "Why didn't you just cut her heart and slice it into little pieces while you were at it?"

"What *I* did?" He jammed his hands into his pockets so he wouldn't shove her back. "I'm the one who walked in and found her snuggled up to that pretty-faced playwright."

"You don't know what you found."

"Then why don't you tell me?"

She'd die first. "You don't know her at all, do you? You didn't have a clue how lucky you were. She's the most loving, most generous, most unselfish person I've ever known. She'd have crawled through broken glass for you." Afraid she'd do something violent if she didn't move, Lori began to pace. "I was so happy when she told me about you. I could see how much in love she was. Really in love. She wasn't just taking you under her wing until she could find someone for you."

"Find someone for me?"

"What do you think she did with all those other men who were dazzled by her?" Lori tossed back. "Oh, she'd try to talk herself into being in love, and thinking they loved her back, and the whole time she'd listen to their problems like some den mother. Then she'd steer them in the direction of some woman she'd decided was perfect for them. She was usually right."

"She was going to marry—"

"She was never going to marry anyone. Whenever she said yes, it was because she couldn't bear to hurt anyone's feelings. And, okay, because she always wanted to have someone she could count on. But however loyal, however sensitive, she is to other people's feelings, she's not stupid. She'd tell herself she was going to get married, then she'd go into overdrive finding the guy a substitute."

"Substitute? Why—?" But Lori wasn't ready to let him get a word in.

"Not that she ever calculated it that way. But after you watched it happen a couple of times, you saw the pattern. But you . . ." She whirled back to him. "You broke the pattern. She needed you. You made her cry." Angry tears glazed Lori's own eyes. "Not once did I ever see her cry over any man. She'd just slip seamlessly into the my-pal-Bess category, and everyone was happy. But she's cried buckets over you.''

He felt sick, and small, and he was beginning to understand a great deal about groveling. "Tell me where she is. Please."

"Why the hell should I?"

"I love her."

She wanted to snarl at him for daring to say so, but she recognized the same misery in his eyes she'd seen in her friend's. "Charlie was—"

"No." He shook his head quickly. "It doesn't matter." What did matter was trust, and it was time he gave it. "I don't need to know. I just need her."

With a sigh, Lori fingered the square-cut diamond on her left hand. Bess had pushed her into taking the right step with Steven. She could only hope she was doing the same in return. "If you hurt her again, Alex—"

"I won't." Then he sighed. "I don't want to hurt her again, but I probably will."

She weakened, because it was exactly the thing a man in love would say. "I sent her home. She wasn't in any shape to work."

"Dyakuyu."

"What?"

"Thanks."

She hated feeling this way. The only way Bess could get from one day to the next was by telling herself it would get better. It had to get better.

But she didn't believe it.

She hadn't had the heart to throw out the lilacs. She'd tried to. She'd even stood holding them over the trash can, weeping like a fool. But the thought of parting with them had been too much. Now she tormented herself with the fragile scent whenever she came downstairs.

She thought about taking a trip—anywhere. She certainly had the vacation time coming, but it didn't seem fair to leave Lori in the lurch, especially since Lori had added wedding plans to her work load.

A lot of good she was doing Lori, or the show, this way, she thought. But the problem of the people in Millbrook seemed terribly petty when compared to hers. Too bad she couldn't write herself out of this one, she thought, as she stood in the kitchen, trying to talk herself into fixing something to eat.

Well, she'd certainly made the grade, Bess told herself, and pressed her fingers against her swollen eyes. She'd fallen in love and had her heart broken. Great research for the next troubled relationship she invented for the television audience.

The hell with food. She was going to go up to bed and will herself to sleep. Tomorrow she would find some way to put her life back together.

When she stepped out of the kitchen, what was left of her life shattered at her feet.

He was standing by the table, one hand brushing over the lilacs. All he did was look at her, turn his head and look, and she nearly crumpled to her knees.

"What are you doing here?" The pain made her voice razor-sharp.

"I still have my key." He lowered his hand slowly. Her eyes were still puffy from her last bout of tears, and there were smudges of fatigue under them. Nothing that had been said to him, nothing he'd said to himself, had lashed more sharply.

"You didn't have to bring it by." If composure was all she had left, she would cling to it. "You could have dropped it in the mail. But thanks." Her smile was so cold it hurt her jaw. "If that's all, I'm in a hurry. I was just on my way up to change before I go out."

"You can't look at me when you lie." He said it half to himself, remembering how her eyes had drifted away from his face when she said she didn't love him.

She forced her gaze back to his, held it steady. "What do you want, Alexi?"

"A great many things. Maybe too many things. But first, for you to forgive me."

Her face crumpled at that. She put a hand up to cover it, knowing it was too late. "Leave me alone."

"*Milaya,* let me—"

"Don't." She cringed away, crossing her arms over herself in self-defense, and his hands stopped an inch away. There was an odd catch in his breath as he drew them back and let them fall to his sides.

"I won't touch you." His voice was quiet and strained. "Please, let me say what I've come to say."

"What else could there be?" She turned away. "I know what you think of me. You made that clear."

"What I did was hurt you and make a fool of myself."

"Oh, yes, you hurt me." She was still trembling from it. "But not just that last time. You hurt me every time you pulled back when I needed to tell you how much I loved you. I thought, I won't let it matter, because he'll have to see it. God, he'll have to see it, because it's right there every time I look at him. Every time I think about him. And he loves me. He wants me. In my whole life, no one wanted me. Not really."

"Bess."

She jerked away from his hands. "My parents," she began, turning back. "How many times I heard them say to each other, 'Where did she come from?' As if I was some stray pet that had wandered in by mistake."

When she began to roam the room, her shoulders still hunched protectively, he said nothing. How could he tell her he was sorry he'd opened up old wounds, and sorry, as well, that it had taken that to have her reveal those smothered feelings to him?

"I handled it." Those stiff shoulders jerked as she tried to shrug it off. "What else could I do? It wasn't their fault, really. They've always been so perfect, in their way, and I could never be. Not for them. Not even for you."

"Do you think that's what I want?"

She glanced back then. The tears had dried up. There was no point in them. "I don't know what you want, Alexi. I only know it keeps circling around. I went from my parents into school. Those awful teenage years, when all the girls were so bright and pretty, and falling in and out of love. No one wanted me. Oh, I had friends. Somewhere along the line I'd learned that if you didn't try so hard, if you just relaxed and acted naturally, that there were a lot of people who'd like you for what you were. But there was never anyone to love. There has never been anybody to love until you."

"There's never going to be anyone else." He waited until she turned back. "I love you, Bess. Please, give me another chance."

"It won't work." She rubbed at her drying tears with the heel of her hand. "I thought it would, I wanted it to. I was so sure love would be enough. But it's not. Not without hope. Certainly not without faith.''

The calm way she said it had panic streaking through him. ''Do you want me to crawl?'' He ignored her defensive retreat and gripped her arms. ''Then I will. You're not going to push me out of your life because I was stupid, because I was afraid. I won't let you.''

Was this how a man crawled? she wondered. With his eyes flashing fire and his voice booming? ''And the next time you see me kissing an old friend?''

''I won't care.'' With a sound of disgust, he released her to stalk the room. ''I will care. I'll kill the next one who touches you.''

''Then New York would be littered with bodies.'' It should be funny, she thought. Why wasn't it funny? ''I can't change what I am for you, Alexi. I wouldn't ask you to change for me.''

''No, you wouldn't.'' He scrubbed his hands over his face and struggled to find some balance. ''I know a kiss between friends is harmless, Bess. I'm not quite that big a fool. But the other night, when I walked in—''

''You assumed I was betraying you.''

''I don't know what I assumed.'' It was as honest as he could get. ''When I saw you, I felt . . . It was all feeling,'' he said carefully. ''So I didn't think. In my heart, in my head, I know better than to assume anything. One of my own rules that I broke. There were reasons.'' Calmer now, he walked back and took her hands. ''We'd just finished the bust, and I was wired from it. I knew I'd tell you about it, all about it. I'd gone beyond trying to separate that part of my life— any part of it—from you. It was going to upset you to think about it, because of Rosalie. I knew that, too. Damn it, I knew you'd gone to that funeral alone, and I felt like the lowest kind of creep for letting you."

He was prying her heart open again, inch by inch. "I didn't think you knew."

"I knew." His voice was flat. All he could think was how desperately he wanted to hold her. "You leave notes everywhere. All these pieces of paper scattered around, with scribbling on them about dry-cleaning and dialogue and appointments. I saw the one about the flowers you'd ordered for her, and the directions to the cemetery." He looked down at their hands. "If things hadn't been moving so fast in the investigation, I would have taken the time. I would have tried to."

That she didn't doubt. "It was more important to me that you catch the man who killed her than that you go stand over her grave."

"I wasn't with you," he said, more slowly. "And I wanted to be. And when I got here, I wanted to..." This was hardly the time to bring up the ring in his pocket. "I was churned up about a lot of things, Bess. My response was way out of line, and I'll apologize for it as often as you like. But I'd like you to hear me out."

"It's all right." She gave his hands a squeeze, hoping he'd release hers. He didn't. "Alexi, Charlie was here because—"

"I don't need to know." Now he let her hands go to bring his own to her face. He wanted her to see what was in his eyes. "You don't have to explain yourself to me. You don't have to change yourself for me."

She felt something move inside her heart and was afraid to believe it was healing. "I'd rather clear the air. I was too angry to do it before. He came by to tell me that Gabrielle was expecting. He was like a little boy at Christmas, and he wanted to share his good news with a friend. And to ask me if I'd be godmother—even though it's seven and a half months down the road."

He lowered his brow to hers. "You should have slugged me, McNee." When he moved his mouth toward hers, he felt her retreat. Patiently he stroked his thumbs over her temples. "Just once," he murmured and tasted her lips.

He didn't mean to deepen the kiss, didn't mean to crush her against him and hold her so tightly neither of them could breathe. But he couldn't stop himself until he felt her body shake with a fresh bout of tears.

"Don't. Please don't." He pressed his face into her hair and rocked her. "I'll break apart."

Turning her face into his shoulder, she fought back the worst of the tears. "I didn't want you to come back. I didn't want to feel this again."

He deserved that, he thought as he squeezed his eyes tight. "You were right to send me away. I want a chance to prove to you that you're right to let me back in." He brushed a hand through her hair. "You're so good at listening, Bess. I have to ask you to listen to me now."

"You don't need to apologize again." She could do nothing but love him, she realized, and, drawing back, she managed a smile. "And I can't let you back in, because you were always here."

Her words brought a pressure to his chest. He pressed their joined hands against it to try to ease it away. "Just that easy?"

"It's not easy." She supposed it would never be easy. "It's just the way it is."

"Mikhail said I would grovel," he murmured. "Bess, you humble me."

"Let's put it behind us." She drew a deep breath, then kissed both his cheeks as a sign of peace. "I'm good at fresh starts."

"No." Taking her hand, he pulled her to the couch. "I like our other start. We don't need a new one, only to play this one out. Sit." He pulled her down with him, keeping her hand close to his heart. "You explained, now I will. I was afraid to believe in you. No woman has ever meant what you mean, and I let myself imagine that you'd be with me forever. Just as I let myself imagine that you'd turn away. And because I was more afraid of the second, it seemed more real."

"It's hard to be afraid." She turned her cheek to her hand. "I know."

"You don't know all." He glanced away, toward the flowers subtly scenting the room. "You kept the lilacs."

"I tried not to." She smiled again. "But they were so beautiful."

"I brought you something besides lilacs that day." He reached into his pocket and drew out the box. Her hand went limp in his. He watched her lips tremble apart. "I don't think it's ostentatious." When she only continued to stare, he shifted. "That was a joke."

"Okay." The two syllables came out in a whisper. "Are you—are you going to let me see it?"

For an answer, he opened the box himself. Inside was a gold band set with a rainbow of gems. He knew what they were only because he'd asked the jeweler to identify each of them. The amethyst, the peridot, the blue topaz, the citrine.

"I know it's not traditional," he said when she remained silent. "But it reminded me of you, and I wanted—hell, I wanted something no one else would have thought to give you."

"No one has," she managed, barely breathing. "No one would."

"If you don't like it, we can look for something else."

She was afraid she would cry again and knew it would do neither of them any good. "It's lovely. Beautiful." She managed to tear her gaze from it. "You bought me this before? You had it with you the other night? You were going to give it to me, then you walked in and saw me with Charlie." Laughing, she lifted a hand to her cheek. "I'm surprised you didn't gun us both down. I couldn't have written it better myself."

"Then you forgive me?"

She already had, but since he was looking so nervous, she nodded. "Anyone with such good taste deserves a second chance."

"I bought this days ago, but it took me a while to work up the nerve. Facing a junkie with an Uzi seemed easier." But he was into it now, and he was going to finish. "My idea was to pressure you to accept it, then push for a quick wedding so you wouldn't change your mind. But that was wrong." He closed the box, and was encouraged by Bess's quick gasp of dismay. "It was stupid, and it showed a lack of faith in both of us. I'm sorry."

"I— You—" She let out a frustrated breath. "I don't mind."

"Of course you do," he said. "It was calculating, even devious, when a proposal of marriage should be romantic. So, when we're both ready, I'll ask you properly."

Her face fell. "When we're both ready?"

"I don't want to push you when you might be feeling a little vulnerable. Especially since a long engagement is out. So I'll give you time."

"Time," she echoed, ready to scream.

"It's fair." He waited a beat. "Okay, I'm ready."

Before she could laugh, he was down on one knee. "What are you doing?"

"A proper proposal of marriage." He nearly launched into his humble little speech. Instead, his eyes darkened when she continued to laugh. "You don't want one."

"Damn right I want one. But I want you up here." She took his hand to tug him back to the couch so that they were at eye level with each other. "I want you to look me right in the eye."

"Okay, then I get something I want, too."

"Name it."

"I want to hear you say it." He caught her hand, brought it to his cheek. "I want very much to hear you say it. I need to hear the words from you."

"I love you, Alexi." For the first time, she said the words smiling, knowing they would be taken as they were meant. "I'm going to love you forever."

He turned his face so that his lips pressed into her palm. Taking the ring out of the box, he slipped it onto her finger. It shot out a rainbow of color. As he linked his fingers with hers, he lifted his head. "Be my family." He shook his head before she could speak and felt himself stumble. "I meant to be romantic. Let me—"

"No." Overwhelmed, she laid a hand over his lips. "That was perfect. Don't change it. Don't change anything."

"Then say yes."

"Yes." She threw her arms around him and laughed. "Oh, yes...."

* * * * *

Silhouette

SPECIAL EDITION®

COMING NEXT MONTH

#877 MYSTERY WIFE—Annette Broadrick

That Special Woman!

Sherye DuBois awoke in a hospital with amnesia—and discovered she was married with children. Could the love of her sexy husband, Raoul DuBois, help to unravel the mystery of her life?

#878 SHADOWS AND LIGHT—Lindsay McKenna

Men of Courage

As a marine, Capt. Craig Taggert had faced many trials. Now his greatest challenge was ahead of him—convincing Lt. Susan Evans that this time, hell or high water wouldn't keep them apart!

#879 LOVING AND GIVING—Gina Ferris

Family Found

Finding his real family was just the first surprise in store for Ryan Kent. True love with the beautiful Taylor Simmons would be the second—and best—discovery of all!

#880 MY BABY, YOUR CHILD—Nikki Benjamin

Everything was at stake when Tess McGuire saved the life of Will Landon's nephew—the child she gave up for adoption. Will's tender, loving care proved he wasn't just grateful, but a man in love....

#881 WALK IN BEAUTY—Ruth Wind

Jessie Callahan never expected Luke Bernali—her lost love and father of her child—to return. But Luke was a changed man, and eager to rekindle a love that never died!

#882 THE PRINCESS OF COLDWATER FLATS
—Natalie Bishop

Single-minded Samantha Whelan's only mission in life was to save her bankrupt ranch. Prairie-tough Cooper Ryan also had designs on the ranch—and on ex-rodeo princess Samantha!

Take 4 bestselling love stories FREE

Plus get a FREE surprise gift!

Special Limited-time Offer

Mail to Silhouette Reader Service™

P.O. Box 609
Fort Erie, Ontario
L2A 5X3

YES! Please send me 4 free Silhouette Special Edition® novels and my free surprise gift. Then send me 6 brand-new novels every month, which I will receive months before they appear in bookstores. Bill me at the low price of $2.96 each plus 25¢ delivery and GST*. That's the complete price and—compared to the cover prices of $3.50 each—quite a bargain! I understand that accepting the books and gift places me under no obligation ever to buy any books. I can always return a shipment and cancel at any time. Even if I never buy another book from Silhouette, the 4 free books and the surprise gift are mine to keep forever.

335 BPA AJJ2

Name	(PLEASE PRINT)	
Address	Apt. No.	
City	Province	Postal Code

This offer is limited to one order per household and not valid to present Silhouette Special Edition® subscribers. *Terms and prices are subject to change without notice.
Canadian residents will be charged applicable provincial taxes and GST.

CSPE-94R   ©1990 Harlequin Enterprises Limited

Are you looking for more titles by
NORA ROBERTS

Don't miss this chance to order additional stories by one of
Silhouette's favorite authors:

Silhouette Intimate Moments®

#07397	+SUZANNA'S SURRENDER	$3.29	☐
#07433	UNFINISHED BUSINESS	$3.39	☐
#07529	°NIGHTSHADE	$3.50	☐

+The Calhoun Women
°American Hero miniseries

Silhouette Special Edition®

#09685	+FOR THE LOVE OF LILAH	$3.29	☐
#09768	*CAPTIVATED	$3.39	☐
#09774	*ENTRANCED	$3.39	☐
#09810	§FALLING FOR RACHEL	$3.39	☐

+The Calhoun Women
*The Donovan Legacy miniseries
§Those Wild Ukrainians miniseries

Silhouette® Books

#48232	†DANCE TO THE PIPER	$2.95	☐

†The O'Hurleys miniseries

Nora Roberts Language of Love

#51001	IRISH THOROUGHBRED	$3.59	☐

(limited quantities available on certain titles)

TOTAL AMOUNT	$	
POSTAGE & HANDLING	$	
($1.00 for one book, 50¢ for each additional)		
APPLICABLE TAXES**	$	_____
TOTAL PAYABLE	$	_____
(check or money order—please do not send cash)		

To order, complete this form and send it, along with a check or money order
for the total above, payable to Silhouette Books, to: **In the U.S.:** 3010 Walden
Avenue, P.O. Box 9077, Buffalo, NY 14269-9077; **In Canada:** P.O. Box 636,
Fort Erie, Ontario, L2A 5X3.

Name: _____

Address: _____ City: _____

State/Prov.: _____ Zip/Postal Code: _____

**New York residents remit applicable sales taxes.
 Canadian residents remit applicable GST and provincial taxes.

Silhouette®

NRBACK2

NORA ROBERTS

Love has a language all its own, and for centuries flowers have symbolized love's finest expression. Discover the language of flowers—and love—in this romantic collection of 48 favorite books by bestselling author Nora Roberts.

Two titles are available every other month at your favorite retail outlet.

In April, look for:

Risky Business Volume #41
Loving Jack Volume #42

In June, look for:

Temptation Volume #43
Best Laid Plans Volume #44

Collect all 48 titles
and become fluent in

THE LANGUAGE of LOVE

Silhouette®

As seen on TV!
Free Gift Offer

With a Free Gift proof-of-purchase from any Silhouette® book,
you can receive a beautiful cubic zirconia pendant.

This gorgeous marquise-shaped stone is a genuine cubic
zirconia—accented by an 18" gold tone necklace.

(Approximate retail value $19.95)

Send for yours today...
compliments of ▼ *Silhouette*®

To receive your free gift, a cubic zirconia pendant, send us one original proof-of-
purchase, photocopies not accepted, from the back of any Silhouette Romance™,
Silhouette Desire®, Silhouette Special Edition®, Silhouette Intimate Moments® or
Silhouette Shadows™ title for January, February or March 1994 at your favorite retail
outlet, together with the Free Gift Certificate, plus a check or money order for $2.50
(do not send cash) to cover postage and handling, payable to Silhouette Free Gift Offer.
We will send you the specified gift. Allow 6 to 8 weeks for delivery. Offer good until
March 31st, 1994 or while quantities last. Offer valid in the U.S. and Canada only.

Free Gift Certificate

Name: _____

Address: _____

City: _____ State/Province: _____ Zip/Postal Code: _____

Mail this certificate, one proof-of-purchase and a check or money order for postage
and handling to: SILHOUETTE FREE GIFT OFFER 1994. In the U.S.: 3010 Walden
Avenue, P.O. Box 9057, Buffalo NY 14269-9057. In Canada: P.O. Box 622, Fort Erie,
Ontario L2Z 5X3

FREE GIFT OFFER   079-KBZ
ONE PROOF-OF-PURCHASE
To collect your fabulous FREE GIFT, a cubic zirconia pendant, you must include this
original proof-of-purchase for each gift with the properly completed Free Gift Certificate.

079-KBZ